Talespin

Sanjay Chopra is a pilot with an international airline and has been flying for the past eighteen years. This has given him the opportunity to explore his interest in the history of various cultures.

He spent enormous amounts of time during his childhood with his grandfather who was a brilliant storyteller and an avid reader, qualities that he inherited. What particularly caught his fancy were the gaps in history, the unknown little details, which have become fodder for his fiction. A course at the London School of Journalism helped him polish his craft.

Of the stories that feature in this collection, 'Turache?' won the Invisible Ink and the Sunpenny publishing contests in the UK; 'A Fate Worse Than' was on the winners' list of the Creative Writers' competition and Southport Writers' Circle; 'Men of the Horse' was on the highly recommended list of The Millennium Writers and Fish Publishing awards; 'The Contractor' was awarded a prize at the Blood Ink Crime Writing Competition, and the entire collection of short stories was in the top five of the Alexander Patterson Cappon Prize for Fiction.

He lives in Mumbai with his wife Tisca Chopra, an actress, with whom he is presently working on a number of film scripts. He is currently working on a novel set in Kashmir, with terrorism providing the backdrop for the action.

Talespin

SANJAY CHOPRA

HarperCollins *Publishers* India

First published in India in 2012 by
HarperCollins *Publishers* India

Building 10, Tower A, 4th Floor, DLF Cyber City, Phase II,
Gurugram Haryana – 122002, India
www.harpercollins.co.in

ISBN: 978-93-5029-368-3

2 4 6 8 10 9 7 5 3 1

Typeset in 11.5/15 Chaparral Pro
Jojy Philip New Delhi 110 015

Printed and bound at
MicroPrints India, New Delhi

To Dr Daisaku Ikeda, my mentor and guide
who taught me that
'where your ability ends, your faith begins.'
To Bauji, my grandfather, who introduced me to the
magical world of storytelling.
Satish and Meena Chopra, my parents, for their
constant love and blessings.
Thank God muses live amongst us in this world, so that
one day we may marry them.
This is for my muse, my wife Tisca.

Contents

To my readers
Stories are an act of collaboration.
Without you, these would be incomplete.

'Turache?'

'He's coming ... He's Coming!'

'Quiet!' Darius thundered.

The trembling messenger fell to the ground and Darius pulled himself back from the boundary of stark blind rage, uneasy at his loss of control.

It's a trap for a king to not seem in control, his father used to say.

'How far away is he?'

'A few miles, Majesty.'

'So the Greek comes ... at last.'

The messenger's wail had startled him. He felt his bladder constrict. The need to relieve himself was overpowering, although he had just been. It had been embarrassingly so since the beginning of this campaign.

'We're ready for him, My Lord. Let him see this place called Gaugamela. Let him see how we've levelled the fields for our chariots. Let him see what he must face tomorrow. Let him feel the fear.' The commander of his chariots had a stooped grey beard. He spoke in the traditional haughty manner of the Persian upper class: jutting his jaw to emphasize each syllable. A manner even Darius's father had affected and something he'd always found irrationally annoying. But the commander spoke with the experience of a dozen successful campaigns.

Not to be outdone, the master of cavalry piped up:

'These Macedonian and Greek ruffians are no match to the splendour of our Persian knights, My Lord!'

The rest of his courtiers immediately took up the cue. He was reminded of hyenas on a carcass.

'Lord of the Celestial Flame, Ahura Mazda has guaranteed our victory, O great Darius!' the high priest yipped, assuring a victory even from the heavens.

He'd gone along with the advice of his court to have this out face-to-face with the Greek. At the council, each and every one of them had bayed for war. Then they had looked back at him, watching, waiting for a reaction. They knew every line, fold and crease on his face. But then, they'd had a lifetime of training to be able to cue into his every expression, he thought.

It was tough, but he managed to declare war with a smile.

'Great Darius! Great Darius!' they started the traditional double clapping and chanting, building it up slowly to a crescendo.

Darius – his royal alias literally meant 'holding on to the good'. The Persian empire, stretching from the Indus to the Ister had been good and much more for three centuries. *Never relinquish your hold on the empire, Son,* his father often said.

He looked at the high priest. He had dressed carelessly today; the sides of his turban were crinkled. There wasn't a court more stylish or elegant than his in all the lands: pleated turbans of scarlet, saffron and purple, tied with robes of blue, emerald green and violet.

But today, his highly fashion-conscious courtiers were slipping. Was there worry beneath the silks and the make-up?

Just because an upstart from the West, eager to gain notoriety, had challenged mighty Persia!

He commanded the greatest armies on this earth, and on this great limitless plain, they would smash the woefully outnumbered Greeks in minutes.

'Bedazzle him first, sire. Invite him for talks and let him see the power and majesty of a real emperor,' his ministers had said.

But now as the moment drew close, he could feel the first throb in his temples. Headaches had been his response to tense situations since childhood. *It's a womanly ailment, Son. Never let your men know of it.* And for years he had followed his father's words and hidden it. But the heat and din of thousands of human bodies living in a camp was worsening his condition. His retainers worked in chain gangs to cool the royal enclosure by soaking reed mats in water and placing them along the walls.

Should he have the giant silver altars that housed the sacred fire removed? Maybe that would bring down the heat in the tent. No, that would be a bad omen. And they certainly added to the grandeur of the scene.

He was following the traditional, tried and tested concept of 'ideal war': assemble a large army, march out and confront the enemy, stun them with pomp and show. And then start negotiations. That was the secret device of the Persians. This was something that other lesser civilizations had no idea about – that riches and wealth could be deadlier than swords and spears.

Bah! Maybe it was all overkill. Maybe he didn't need any of it, even this meeting. This Greek, this nobody, was probably already regretting having challenged the Persian empire.

How he wished he could be back in Persepolis, in civilization, with what he loved best, his musical orchestras and his gardens. They were firdu ... his paradise. Designed and built by his forefathers, the city and the palace were beacons of culture. That was where he came from, a grand legacy of great kings. What were the credentials of this brat? Just ignorance and youth!

What did the young know about tradition, culture, the running of an empire? All they had was hunger and the thought that the world owed it to them to satiate it.

Well this was one youngster who would find reality on that field tomorrow, unless of course, he came to his senses after the meeting today. Then he would forgive the Greek. *Generosity and especially its very public demonstration are great qualities for a king.* He remembered his father's words.

'He is here, Majesty!' someone cried from outside.

Darius rose from his travelling cedar-wood throne, baffled.

He is here?

But he hadn't heard any sounds of trumpets or cymbals or even vocal announcements, the traditional way of ushering aristocracy. No fanfare? Did he not know any protocol?

The flap of the outer tent that formed a reception area flipped open and he caught a glimpse through the dust of men and horses, leather and bronze.

As he went closer, the group of men came in walking fast, almost strutting ... like common soldiers. Very unlike the dignified, measured steps he was taking.

The entire assembly in the tent rose and bowed low to Darius and then turned to face the visitors. His interpreter moved up to his side. The band of men stopped a few feet away. They were all dressed alike in bronze, iron armour and helmets. There wasn't a piece of silk or gold on them.

The one leading the company had ostrich feathers on his helmet, which he took off to reveal wild golden curls.

His empire spanned twelve races, but never before had Darius seen such a group of men. Their clothing was simple, their hair unkempt, and they smelt ... of horses! These people, this man, had come to challenge Persia?

His face framed by his long, unruly locks seemed like a boy's. Darius felt his head begin a manic drumbeat.

The irritation he thought he had subdued earlier left him short of breath.

The Persian interpreter began the ritual chant to introduce an emperor. But Darius felt compelled to intervene. The first words must be his, to show this *boy* what he thought of his feeble attempt at being a king. He swept the interpreter aside. His words should carry the essence of his superiority, he thought, his introduction as it was meant to be – an emperor, the light of the universe.

He spoke in Persian, the only language fit for a royal.

He didn't know why or where the words came from, but when they did, they sounded like a high-pitched cry.

'Pidram sultan bood!' (My forefathers were great kings!)

It was to be a challenge, a battle cry, a claim of lineage and heritage thrown in the face of the Greek.

Then Darius saw the face of the boy. It was calm. Utterly, irritatingly calm. The Greek interpreter started to translate, but the boy silenced him. He looked at Darius and spoke.

It was a question asked in the same language Darius had used ... Persian!

'Turache? Turache?' (Who are you?)

The entire gathering stood still. Sound, it seemed, had been sucked out of the enclosure. No one had ever spoken to the Emperor this way.

Darius was stunned. This Greek spoke Persian? Just how much did he know about them?

Who are you? Darius realized in that instant that it was a question he had shied away from his entire life. Who was he? What was his own identity? All this glory was just inherited. Even his name was taken from an ancestor's.

The Greek's words left him feeling naked, his core exposed. The moment was slipping from his hands, he must find a suitable repartee, he must have the last word.

A king must have the last word, his father's words resounded.

Oh! Let me be now, Pader ... let me have some original thoughts, not just second-hand words of a long-dead ancestor. He almost shouted his thoughts aloud. For the first time, Darius felt his ancestry to be a burden, an encumbrance.

But nothing came out of him. His life force seemed drained. The need to relieve his bladder had become a burning agony now.

The Persian interpreter, confused by this unorthodox exchange, decided to finish the introduction.

'There stands before you, O Lord Darius, Alexander, the prince of Macedonia.'

Darius looked into the boy's eyes. He stepped back as if physically struck. They blazed with a power he had never seen in a human. Like a dark, deep force of nature, a high wind that blows across the earth, sweeping all before it, uncompromising. It was folly to think he could have negotiated with this man. For how do you negotiate with a hurricane?

When he had heard stories of a force coming from the West, he had imagined an army, troops and cavalry. Now he knew that the force was what lay in the eyes of just one man and it was ... indefatigable.

He wished he was far away from what lay on the plains of Gaugamela the next day. He knew suddenly that no matter what his generals said or how enormous the odds in his favour, the battle was lost today to that one question: who are you?

His father had often compared life to a poem. If so, would his contributing verse be failure?

Yah Mazda! Even now he couldn't get his father's words out of his head.

Later, he sat alone for hours, shunning the company of his court and harem. When it was dark, he went out into the open to be away from the camp. His numb senses carried him faster and faster. He could hear jackals yipping in the distance. Then suddenly a lone one far away howled a long plaintive cry. Pidram sultan bood, Pidram sultan bood, it seemed to go. And the westerly wind sweeping the plains, as if in reply mocked again and again ... 'Turache? Turache?'

Darius stopped, unable to find an answer.

Note: In October 331 BC, on the plains of Gaugamela, Darius with an army of 2,50,000 faced Alexander's modest force of 45,000 soldiers. The battle ended with Darius fleeing the field. The Persian empire collapsed and Alexander gained access to Asia. Unknown to the players themselves, the stakes here were nothing short of world dominance. The Battle of Gaugamela changed the map of the world. Before this time, the eastern empires had dominated the world stage. After this battle, the ascendancy of the West was secure.

A Fate Worse Than

The tip of the Mongol spear pierced the small of my back. The Uzbeks had no reason to be gentle and I had stopped expecting it years ago. I was not worthy of their respect. For you see, not only am I a prisoner, but also an infidel – the kind the followers of the Prophet despise the most. I am what they call a Yehudi ... a Jew.

They led me across a river that was frozen like all the others we had crossed, but now the men were tired and cold. A thousand little fires sprang up beside the river and the men pushed and shoved to get close to them. My lord had found a new foe: winter. This was no war, it had become a personal duel, and some said no matter how many fell, he would not call a halt.

But here at Otrar, still months away from China, winter had forced him to stop. There were rumours that he was gravely ill. He had taken refuge in the palace of Amir Beg, one of his underlings. That was where the guards were taking me.

Lowly court officers lived in better dwellings in Samarkhand. How my lord would have hated to be housed here!

I had last been in Timur's presence months back. The wrinkled figure that lay shivering in his own sweat looked like a ghostly shadow now. Nobles and court physicians crowded around him.

'Why does he summon the Yehudi?' someone whispered.

I went to my lord's bedside and bent low. His booming voice had been reduced to a whisper. I had to stoop till my ear was near his face. He suddenly clutched at my tunic with both hands. I was in a sweat myself. I'd never been so close to the emperor. He had shooed the others away. His words were to be private. Blood-splattered spittle coated his beard.

'I'm dying, Yehudi ... I know it. I've been good to you, haven't I?'

His eyes still retained their customary fire.

I was on my knees, trembling in his weakening grasp, transported instantly to my native city, Sivas. Thousands buried alive, the blackened streets, the pyramids of heads. Just another typical Timurid conquest. He had slaughtered many, but spared me as he did all artisans who could be put to use in his beloved Samarkhand. Never had I been more grateful for the magic that resides in my hands. And may God forgive my vanity, but I was the best engraver and calligrapher in all the lands.

'I need your art ... your last task. Engrave a phrase on my tomb ... something to warn posterity ... something to keep those who dared not touch me while I am alive from defiling me when I'm dead. I know there are many who are waiting to settle scores. The words should keep the robbers of tombs away ... forever. Make the words terrible and the engraving beautiful. For if my eternal solitude is disturbed ...'

The ranting suddenly stopped. His voice became a whisper.

'I've never treated your people badly, huh?'

That was true, my master had treated all people equally ill, regardless of race or religion.

'But if you don't do as I say, I will seek vengeance from all humanity … and especially your people!'

The effort of speaking was too much, he fell back, and with a spluttering sound his bowels voided and the great Timur lay back gasping on his befouled furs.

They hurried me out, swathed me with blankets and found me a good horse and an escort. I had to be kept safe till I reached Samarkhand.

He was dying. I couldn't believe it. Timur the terrible, the scourge of Asia, demon to some, emperor to others … dying!

I didn't know what to feel. I'd been a captive for too many years and he had been my master for too long.

'Make the words terrible and the engraving beautiful,' he had said. And that was my lord, terrible and beautiful at the same time. A ruthless killer and an ardent patron of the arts. He was a besotted lover of his Samarkhand. The city, like a greedy mistress, had sent him out again and again to conquer more and more. And now he was dying far from his beloved, with no hope of seeing her again.

I buried my hands deeper into my blanket. They must be preserved for the task ahead. The inscription on his tomb would be verses from the Koran, but I had never been allowed to carve sacred lines from it before – my kaffir hands could pollute their pure belief. That did not stop him from selecting me. Timur was secular when it suited him. He had me work on the arched gates at Chinar gardens and his blue palace. The better-cut inscriptions extolling the virtues of the emperor were all mine.

The responsibility was overwhelming. What could possibly be engraved on my master's tomb to stay the hand of mankind from touching his grave ... forever?

That was his command and I believed him; his wrath was terrible enough to strike from the great beyond. But it was not wrath alone, for what I'd just seen in my master's eyes was ... fear. Those eyes seemed to mirror his life's work: dozens of burnt cities, hundreds of thousands of slaughtered humans and untold misery.

The great lord was scared of what lay on the other side, just like any of us. He was a follower of Allah, but nomadic enough at heart to dread the afterlife and believe in charms and curses. His ancestors, Mongol chieftains, had been extremely secretive about their burial places. None of their burial sites had ever been discovered. However, the Islamic tradition was to make burials grand, to celebrate greatness or sometimes bestow it upon the dead by way of pomp and show. Clearly my master was torn between the two loyalties of wanton nomad and sombre Muslim coursing through his blood. And he had chosen both!

The beards of my fellow riders were frosted over, but the chill I felt in my bones was not just from the cold. I had to ensure that generations to follow were safe from Timurid savagery, the kind that I had seen inflicted on my people and others.

The walls of the magnificent city were in my sight when I got the inspiration. I would use the archaic Uzbek script. I loved its stylized appearance, its whorls and loops. For a moment, a doubt crept in. Would commoners readily understand it? Maybe I could engrave a second line, a translation. Yes!

That's how I'd do it. And I would use the name of my lord as a threat to all. For what could be more terrifying than Timur himself?

I moved towards the heart of the structure into the dark interior of my lord's last resting place. Hundreds of workmen were occupied in the frantic construction. I made my way to the onyx-tiled wall, to the spot where Koranic inscriptions covered the wall.

There, just above the tomb itself was my work, standing out in its sheer artistry. I was now ready to etch the translation, the second line. I heard a voice behind me and saw Mahmoud Isfahni, the royal architect, making his way across the hall.

'Yehudi! You were commissioned to work just one line. The rest of the wall space is needed for other inscriptions. Gather up your tools and be gone!'

I did not even protest. My protection had died with my lord. Isfahni was a Sheikh and I was still a slave. Before he could lose his temper, I was gone.

Brigadier Igor Antonov took another sip of the over-sweetened tea and sighed. It was going to be a long wait.

He rose from the solid block of masonry and stretched himself to his full six foot two. They had been camping in Samarkhand for days, right in the middle of the old quarter, the Registan, in full view of the cupola of the Gur-e Amir, the mausoleum of Timur. He had been lucky to wangle a place in the team of the great archaeologist Mikhail Gerasimov himself.

Though a full-time army man, archaeology was his passion and this trip had exceeded all expectations. The methods of Dr Gerasimov had been a revelation. History's greatest mass murderer, Timur the terrible, was the subject of Dr Gerasimov's study. His meticulous research had enabled them to go beyond the ornately carved façade and discover the secret tomb of Timur.

The body had been exhumed and was to be taken to Moscow. Tufts of red hair confirmed the myth of the barbarian's 'blazing countenance'. Dr Gerasimov wanted to verify that Timur had indeed been lame and was related in lineage to that other great Mongol, Chengez Khan.

The expedition was at an end. Everything recovered from the area of the tomb was neatly catalogued and packed in wooden cases to be sent to the museum in Moscow. The work was done, all the loose ends tied. All except one, that is. The blue-and-white tiled wall around the tomb had verses from the Koran cut into it, but just above the other Islamic mosaics was one line engraved deeper and darker than the rest. Trouble was, nobody, not even their expert on Uzbek languages, could decipher the script.

It had taken them days to find someone who could figure it out. It was apparently written in the ancient Uzbek script, very rare and so old that it had become obsolete even in Timur's time. They were still in there, trying to crack that one line. He was ready to ignore it and walk away, but not Dr Gerasimov. The doctor was not leaving till it was over and only the doctor decided when that was.

He lit a cigarette and flipped open a newspaper. It was a copy of the *Pravda* dated 20 June 1941 – the papers reached these provinces a couple of days late. It was the same story, crop failures and purges ordered by comrade Stalin ... they were targeting the army top brass now. Stalin's insecurities were ruining the Red Army. Nobody knew when the goons would arrive to pack them off to Siberia.

He threw down the paper in disgust.

The other reading material at hand was a Red Army study on the comparative performance of tanks. Igor commanded a brigade of Russian T-30 tanks based in Ukraine. Soon he was absorbed in the report. The study concluded that though the Russian T-30 was a match for the British Sherman, it was woefully inadequate compared to the German Tiger tank. The report was worrying and Igor was still thinking about it when Dr Gerasimov walked in with the Ukranian translator and his staff.

The beaming faces told him that they had successfully deciphered the phrase atop Timur's tomb. One of the assistants held out a sheet of paper. It read: *A fate worse than me will befall anyone who dares disturb me*.

Only later did Igor realize that the coldness in his chest must have been a premonition. He looked at the other faces – not one registered worry. He read the line again.

A fate worse than me ... and not mine. The menace was unmistakable. Why couldn't the others see it?

The far-off sound he had been hearing became an engine beat. They all looked in the direction of the road and around the mound of rubble appeared a goggled and helmeted figure on a motorcycle. The dispatch rider leapt off the bike and came to attention in front of Igor. He held out a dirt-stained paper.

'Urgent message from Moscow, Brigadier.'

Igor was puzzled. His leave was good for another week. He tore open the envelope.

22 June 1941
To Brigadier Igor Antonov,

Rejoin your unit with extreme, repeat extreme urgency. German army formations have attacked across the whole front. Two divisions of Tiger tanks reported to be heading towards your unit.

Army Headquarters,
Moscow

Igor read the message again and sat down, stunned. The lines seemed to blur. Only one message stood out clearly.

'A fate worse than me,' Timur had said.

Note: Hitler's attack on Russia, code-named 'Operation Barbarossa', killed 25 million people – the highest casualty figure in any war in history. An estimated two million of these were Jews. The Soviet government finally decided to bury Timur's body back in the mausoleum at Samarkhand.

Men of the Horse

'Be men!' Odysseus bellowed.

The sweaty faces of the warriors grinned as one. They knew what would come next.

'Keep your swords up!'

'Like men!' they yelled back in unison.

Odysseus locked his face in a scowl. They would be watching him and he didn't want them to see the surge of affection he felt for them. He sharpened his tone.

'Lock your shields, slow tread!'

Shields rasped close, interlocked, the platoon moved on tiptoe as if stepping on hot stones. Their formation looked like a large armoured porcupine, the swords its quills.

These fervent exercises had been going on for a fortnight now. They drilled all night on the beach till the eastern sky turned a shade and the grey cliffs started taking shape. Only then did they stop and slip away to the Greek encampment. Exhausted, they breakfasted on sweet corn bread and milk, and dropped on their sleeping mats.

The castle gleamed in the morning light, its limestone walls taunting the Greeks who, for the last ten years, had been gnawing away at its belly. Even so, after countless bloody assaults, the city's flag blew in the wind, bold and free.

The Greek rolls appeared like a veritable who's who of the Bronze Age. Champions like Achilles, Ajax, Diomedes and Odysseus, heroes who could scatter the enemy like chaff and inspire their men to follow them to the gates of hell if necessary. They could summon the gods at will. They were big and cruel and rapacious. And yet they could not breach this city. Even after ten years, Troy stood firm.

Neel Batra felt the tension in the room as he got up to speak. The gathering here made the Archaeological Survey of India seem like pre-school. This was serious stuff. The International Society of Troy. It was the first time he was presenting a paper at this level. Nothing in his years of army service had scared him as much. But this had been a dream and he was living it, finally. He had always wanted to be connected to history and archaeology, ever since he saw the first *Indiana Jones* movie as a boy. The years spent in the army had been an obligation fulfilled for the sake of his family, his father.

'The men in this family have been serving the army for generations, Son. It is what we do. My old regiment is waiting for you, Neel. It will make me very proud when you join them.'

This was the first time Baba had ever asked him for anything. His extended family had never tired of praising his father; ever since he could remember, his cousins ranging from four to forty years never left their home without comics, dinky cars, in some cases money or job recommendations. Major General Batra was commonly known to be the most magnanimous man in their circle.

And Baba had always pampered Neel to the point of spoiling him, his old aunts had cautioned whoever was listening. But Baba didn't care, he went right ahead, never refusing him anything. His childhood had been filled with parties and picnics, toys and happy memories. That was many years before Neel had realized that his father was essentially a soft man who had an overwhelming need for approval, whose very existence depended on the need to be needed.

Neel lived with the constant fear that he might inherit even a fraction of this eager-to-please nature from his father. Baba was an old man now, holding onto trophies dulled by time, peering suspiciously into the future. He no longer had much to give and so the steady flow of visitors had dried to a trickle.

Neel knew he would give in to Baba's wishes. He had realized early on that he had inherited his father's non-confrontational nature. The odds of getting the better of such emotional blackmail were few. But his heart was just not in it. He remembered being eighteen and feeling raw and fragile on the long train ride to the military academy. To his relief he'd made a good soldier, albeit a reluctant one.

All his life Neel had been told about how his father had got the Vir Chakra, one of the military's highest honours, for his bravery. Baba rarely mentioned the medal himself. Maybe his self-effacing nature didn't allow him to boast about it. In the 1971 war, his father had led a small platoon of troops and some local Bangladeshi guides and overrun an entire line of machine gun nests.

For Neel promotions had arrived on time till one day an operation against militants had been badly botched up. The top brass neatly evaded the heat and the axe came down on the company commander. That man was Neel. Friends and colleagues had advised him to challenge the verdict, but Neel knew that the odds were against him. So when a soft option – early retirement – was offered, he took it. All debts to his father and family name were settled, he decided that now it was time to follow his childhood passion.

So here he was. A rookie archaeologist amongst the biggest names in the world. His first presentation, and he was going to burst their bubble.

They did not even wait for him to finish. Young and eager, stooped and grey, they fell upon him as one. The host speaker flailed his reedy arms like a bird to silence them. Neel was expecting this. After all, these were the same people who had announced to the world a year ago that they now had the answer to the age-old riddle.

They had announced that the ancient city of Troy had indeed fallen to that great Greek deception, the wooden horse, and the latest evidence emerging from the site of Troy at Hissarlik in Turkey clinched it. The media had gone wild and the world had celebrated their findings. Academic laureates and lavish funding had followed.

In spite of the host's fervent appeals, the hall looked and sounded like a factory workers' union meet. Professor Scheider took his elbow and led him out.

'It was bound to happen, let them settle down. Maybe you could come back in later.'

The professor, himself an expert researcher on Troy, was the only one supporting Neel's theory, or at least the only one willing to hear it. He had arranged for Neel to present his paper.

'Don't worry, Neel, I'll answer their questions. I know your paper well enough.'

He did and Neel knew that the professor would be much more professional at fielding questions. But he'd hoped that it would be him in there, hobnobbing with the pundits, rubbing shoulders with genius. The professor may have had some ulterior motive in this. After all, when the Trojan horse excavation had been unveiled, Scheider's team had not been a part of it. And in the intensely competitive world of top-notch archaeology, no one would share a nub of credit. Maybe he was the professor's revenge.

The International Society of Troy's A-team had hit upon a treasure trove a year ago. In an obscure part of the diggings at Troy, preserved over the centuries in surprisingly good condition, were the remnants of a large wooden horse. And next to it, clay tablets depicting the now well-known tale in chilling detail. Here, then, was the answer to that great debate. Homer had been right. Troy had indeed fallen to the famous Greek trick – the Trojan horse!

Neel, as part of his research scholarship, had chosen an international project. Troy came to him by pure chance. One of the conditions for funding by the UN was that the team working on it should be an international one. There was no representation from India. His application was accepted to give the project the required 'international flavour'. He would not be given any serious research to do. His job was to sign on the dotted line below 200 others who made up the team. He knew that he was just a rubber stamp, but he didn't care. He needed an escape from the dreary government offices and from his home. Troy was a hot project and about to get hotter. Neel's specialty was military history and quite by accident he had stumbled upon a huge flaw in their theory.

Halle, Neel's half-Turkish assistant, tossed back her lovely head. She was thrilled at his defiance of authority.

'Their faces looked like they were going to explode. You really shook their uptight world!'

Halle was a great secretary, a computer wiz, and a treat to look at. And he, well, he was married.

'Tell me again, Neel ... Just in case I get cornered by the press.' She was practically cooing and Neel was not above her charms.

He grinned. 'Okay. The Society's claim last year about the horse and the fall of Troy is based on one key assumption. You know, the legend says that the horse carried within it a number of Greek soldiers. While Troy celebrated the departure of the Greeks, these men opened the gates from the inside and let in the rest of the Greek army which was hiding out of view.

'Now that's what the world believed, but I started my research by looking at this story from a different angle. You see, I have been in the army and have trained many commandoes. I asked myself, how many Greek soldiers would be required for an operation like this? I looked at the city of Troy – the size of their force, the number of gates, etc. and arrived at a minimum number. That number, according to my calculation, is ten.

'Sure, it can be argued that the Trojans gave themselves up to a night of wild revelry. Surprise, night-time and Trojan drunkenness would have given the Greeks an advantage. But don't forget, the Trojans were warriors who had fought off the Greeks for ten years. They would never have completely dropped their guard. So a bare minimum of ten Greeks would have been required in that horse to fight off the guards and open the gates. And therein lies the problem. It is easy to calculate the dimensions of the Trojan horse from its remains and the information on the tablets. Such a structure could not have accommodated ten, fully-armed men, even if they were folded double. So now, that is the Society's predicament.

'They've taken great pains to prove to the world that this was the very same horse that the Greeks used. Either they take back that claim or the story goes back to its old status that it's all just an over-hyped myth and there's no proof that any of it ever happened.'

King Agamemnon looks at the assembly of his chiefs. The lamps throw eerie patterns around the tent and the light hides more than it reveals. It doesn't, however, hide the exhaustion and frustration on their faces. Except for Menelaus, whose eyes still glow with rage. It's a rage that has not waned in ten years. Helen, his wife, still resides safe in the citadel of Troy with her lover, Paris.

Odysseus shrugs off his heavy woollen cloak. His face is, as usual, an inscrutable mask. He is known more as a master of strategy and deception than a hardcore, bone-shattering warrior.

Agamemnon breaks the silence. 'I ask you again. Are you sure it can be done?'

Odysseus knows why the question is being asked repeatedly in front of others. So that in case of failure, there will be a readymade scapegoat. He doesn't mind. This is how politics works.

He gets to his feet, ready to launch into his famous oratory, but the faces of the men around him make him rethink. These are men who have been away from home and love for ten long years. They deserve rest, and the truth. He speaks quietly and with confidence.

'It will work, milord. I've trained the team myself, but apart from that, do we have a choice? For ten years we've bled an entire generation of Greeks and yet have come nowhere closer. Achilles and his fierce troops can never scale these walls, nor can our other chiefs.'

It works. This statement a few years back would have evoked strong protests, even abuse. But now not a squeak can be heard from the company. No one has the stomach or the stamina for any more pitched battles. One by one they raise their hands to show acceptance of the plan.

Epecius, the master craftsman, then presents a clay model of the beast. It will be made of pinewood, its eyes amber, teeth ivory and crest of real horsehair. It is to be an irresistible gift and an offering to goddess Athena. And in its belly it will carry its deadly cargo.

Neel's cellphone rang. He looked up from his laptop. The customized 'wife calling' ringtone which had made him smile till a few years ago, had now begun to annoy him. He was losing Priya – not to another man, that would be easier somehow. She was changing into someone he couldn't connect with and he missed her, sometimes even when she was in the same room. That irritated him. And always made him feel guilty at being irritated.

Perhaps a child would have helped. That, in any case, had been the plan. But Priya's miscarriage had pushed things deeper into the abyss. And she had not tried to heal either, almost nursing her trauma. It was tearing them apart. Each occupied a side of the bed and a void rested between them, a living thing, almost as real as their lost child.

His salvation lay in immersing himself in his work while her thing had been to hoist herself aboard every cocktail-drenched, socialite-studded charity, as long as it had something to do with children. Her disappointments were many and they only added to her depression. Most of these charities were just social clubs where after the champagne and five-star buffet bills had been paid, there was precious little left to help anyone. That didn't stop her though. She had a lavish trust fund set up by her grandfather and she squandered it away to buy that most elusive commodity – peace of mind.

As usual, the phone call started without any preliminaries. It was about this new organization which rescued children working in sweatshops in India. She had just visited an unlicensed carpet factory a couple of hundred miles from Delhi.

'It was horrible, Neel. These kids are barely ten years old. They prefer children because only their fingers can weave the really delicate patterns. Like the rug we have in the living room. I've given it away ... couldn't bear to look at it. They had those kids tied to the looms. How can they do this?' She started sobbing.

Neel was surprised. This was the first time she had gone beyond the cocktail luncheon circuit.

'It's been a long time, Neel. I want to see you. Can you get away for a few days?'

He detected shades of the old Priya. Even though it was the most inconvenient time work-wise, he wished he could meet her and listen to her quick mind dissect his problems. He missed her smile and the way she rubbed his temples when he was tired. She'd been his constant support in the 'wilderness years'. He asked her to fly down to Istanbul.

The following week, on a rain-drenched morning, the digs at Troy regurgitated their final treasure and last secret. A baked clay tablet inlaid with copper. Etched clearly on it were the words: 'Men of the Horse'. And listed there were the names of the heroes of the Trojan horse. There were five names on one side and five on the other.

Neel was urgently summoned to the director's office.

The find had put his theory of ten warriors right up there in the 'brilliant' category. Professor Scheider was present as well and had an offer for him: he was to announce that his calculations had been wrong earlier and bury his 'ten warriors cannot fit in this contraption' theory. In return, a doctorate and a lucrative, high visibility but low accountability job as a consultant. They were offering him a dream. A doctorate on a platter and a chance to work abroad, escape the musty offices of the Archaeological Survey of India.

They gave him the weekend to decide. But he was sure he didn't need that much time to say yes. After all, the purpose of his research was to be officially decorated and financially secure. Who cared what had happened to a dead civilization thousands of years ago? What the hell, it wasn't even his civilization. He had left the army willingly, but if he became pig-headed about this research, he would be forcibly evicted from this job as well. Branded a loser forever.

Suddenly he remembered his instructor from the army commando school. They were setting off on a forty-mile hike with a full kit. Half the distance would be covered carrying their partners, to simulate an injured comrade. The last five miles were a killing climb up a steep hillside. The entire training till this point had been about building stamina and strength. Then the instructor spoke:

'You will find, gentlemen, that in the last few miles your stamina, endurance and strength will fail you. What will get you over that hill will eventually be your character and integrity.'

As an afterthought he added, 'These will get you over most hills in life as well.'

He remembered the old battle-scarred colonel clearly. Was that old lecture still valid? Had it ever been valid or was it just bullshit fed to the youth to make them finish courses, charge into battle, face shrapnel and bullets and plant flags on lonely hills or reject ready-made doctorates? He wouldn't be sucker enough to fall for that crap. He would put his papers to the shredder. A drifter no more, he would embrace success.

The priest utters the last few words of prayer to Ares, the god of war. They are clad in bronze and leather, short swords at their sides, the bows taut and quivers fat. Agamemnon stops to pat a shoulder or tousle a head as he passes them.

'We have had many heroes in this war, but that has not brought us success. I bless your venture. I have ordered the royal scribe to record your names so that you may become immortal. For you are real men and will from now be called "Men of the Horse".'

The assembly rang with loud cheering and whoops of delight. Their hearts sang and chests swelled when the king called them 'real men'.

They were sitting in a sidewalk café in Istanbul, within sight of the famous blue mosque. It was the last of the glorious days of sunshine before the winds picked up over the Bosphoros straits and stormed the city with rain. Priya was telling him about the hovels she had visited.

'I want to save them, Neel, but I don't know how.'

Well, he didn't either.

He had enough confusions of his own to deal with. Should he sell out on his research and take the goddamn doctorate? His pent-up dilemma spilled out untidily, but he knew she understood.

'What is it that you want,' she began, when a commotion on the street interrupted them.

A couple of kids were kicking a ball. A smaller boy, who was leading a puppy on a string, skipped down the street. One of the older boys suddenly knocked him down and started kicking the puppy. Yelling, the other kids joined in, kicking the child and the puppy in turn. The café owner screamed at them.

Priya looked back at Neel. 'God! Kids can be monsters too! I mean, even to each other. The weavers divide them up in gangs according to their caste and pit the teams against each other. They make a sport out of it and those kids go on and on for sixteen hours a day to earn ten rupees. Sometimes, during breaks, they get into bloody fights with each other. The weavers encourage this. It keeps their spirits up, they say. Do you know, in some places in Africa and Asia, they use children as soldiers. I read an interview of a guerilla commander who said that they make the best soldiers. They don't ask questions, they work for a pittance and treat everything as a game.'

Neel was listening now.

'You've been so long in the army, Neel, but I'm sure

you don't know this. Some people believe that the word infantry comes from a band of infants or child soldiers.'

He was on his feet. He ran. As fast as his legs could carry him. At the hotel, he switched on his laptop and fed in some new numbers. He waited breathlessly for the result. It lit up on his screen a second later. TEN!

When Priya came in, he told her what he'd discovered.

'Are you still confused, Neel? I mean, it's clear, isn't it? This is what you've wanted for so long. They're giving it to you on a plate. That doctorate will really make you. You stand to gain the world and lose nothing ... Just your soul.'

She said that simply, with the confidence and clarity of the girl he'd met years ago.

She had said it to him before, he remembered, when the army had charged him with dereliction of duty. She had wanted him to make a stand, but he had copped out ... all his life.

He nodded and reached for his cellphone.

All his life he had admired the ancients, especially the Greeks. He'd worshipped the romance and tragedy in their tales. He'd believed that only in those times had men been truly glorious. Troy had been their greatest conquest. And it had been won not by their much feted champions, but by warriors of a much smaller stature. He felt betrayed – like a child. A victim of another exposed fairy tale. A pawn used to fix problems in the world of grown-ups.

His head throbbed, like it had all those years back when on deputation to army intelligence, he'd accidentally come across an old file in the records office. Photographs of mutilated and bullet-ridden corpses of children and a report dated December 1971.

The kids were local Bangladeshi guides. An officer of the Ranger's Regiment had been ordered to clear out machine gun posts on a hill. The officer had hit upon a brilliant idea. Send the kids ahead at night to overcome the sentries, to be used as cannon fodder. The children actually managed to clear out the hill. They'd died in the process, each one of them. Innocent flesh easily ripped apart by the heavy machine guns.

Naturally, the army had covered up the incident. And to complete the cover up, they awarded the officer in charge a Vir Chakra.

His hands shook as he turned to the photograph and the last page. There was his father standing atop a hill, flag in hand. A familiar, pleasing smile in place. The handiwork of a 'very nice man'.

He'd once read a newspaper article about how some records of that war had gone missing. He didn't know now whether they were deliberately 'misplaced' or genuinely lost, buried in what seemed like acres of paper.

Neel had shredded the file. The army's shame all those years back had hushed up the incident; his own could not bear it, even in an old forgotten file.

For weeks he couldn't sleep. Even now he felt a sense of dread when alone with his father.

Neel realized that since the day he saw the photos of those corpses of Bangladeshi kids, he'd been peering into a dark alley. It was time to enter it. This is what the old colonel meant when he said that some things are worth fighting for. He realized that for the first time, the odds didn't frighten him.

The noises of wild merry-making from outside have died down. They sit motionless in the deep darkness. Odysseus, their leader, was named after the great hero who has trained them. He strikes a flint and lights the slow torch.

'Come,' he says. 'It is time.'

'For glory!' he says, pulling his sword from the scabbard.

'For glory!' they whisper back, touching his sword with theirs.

He holds the torch up and their faces swim into view, gleaming with mischief. He unhinges the trapdoor and lowers the rope. It is his duty to lead them down. For, at fourteen years, he is the eldest in the band and their leader. The wraith-like figures slide down the rope from the disembowelled horse. Each child sharp as a finely-honed arrow and named after a hero of this war. Ajax, Acamas, Echion, Megases ... They are here to avenge their forefathers. Troy is doomed.

Awake

Magadha, 500 BC.

A series of revolts break out in the copper and iron mines of the northern states against the imperialist control of Emperor Ajatashatru.

Mara waited till they were all in position, then brought his arm down. The royal trumpeters blared a signal to the hundred chariots.

Clicks of reins and flails and they were off.

They swept outward and around the yelling horde of rebels, just outside the range of their arrows and catapults.

It was a manoeuvre supposedly handed down by the gods. His Aryan ancestors called it the chakravyuh, the whirling disc. In a thousand years, no one had broken it.

It was an equestrian ballet.

Each alternate chariot bore a warrior armed with bow, lance and sword, and every fourth one with a battle axe.

Shoot thrust slash chop – thrust slash thrust chop.

The formation moved, spinning like a disc. By the time you engaged one warrior, he'd already moved on, leaving you to face another one. A powerful whirlpool, it sucked up everything in its path, regurgitating the debris of men, metal and horse.

Moving, whirling in rhythm to the incessant beat of the kettle drums.

Thud! Thud! Thud! Like the throb of some giant beast's heart.

And that's what this manoeuvre made of men – numb beasts, like oxen yoked to a train. Wasn't that why it worked so well? Numb the warrior, don't let him think. Make him part of a machine. A machine free from human error. Take error out of war – take human out of war.

He stumbled over his own thoughts. In all these years, never once had he thought about it this way.

What was wrong with him? Since when had his mind become so loud?

The last act was now underway. The giant pincers of the trap opened up, exposing him invitingly, luring the enemy.

Their leader was not a warrior, he had just supplied the ideology for this revolt. The angered miners and villages on the border had found an answer to years of dissatisfaction with Ajatashatru's Magadha. This firebrand youth had promised a newer, better life by breaking away from Magadha. He now stood frozen, his enthusiasm dampening by the mayhem and the sight of his fast-depleting force.

But his aide was a warrior. Mara had picked him out at first glance. He turned his chariot towards Mara and charged. A few of his men tried to follow, but the pincers of the chakravyuh closed with a thunderclap of steel on bone and bridle.

Mara could never understand it when others told him

that everything seemed to flash past in the heat of battle. To him time always seemed to slow down; each sound and colour appeared to stand out in combat. He could pinpoint the moment when the young warrior realized his companions had been left behind. He saw the despair on his face, the dread of being alone. He saw the struggle of the young warrior to replace naked fear with cold courage.

Wear one mask in exchange for another.

Mara felt sweat form on his brow under the iron mask. It was a hot day, but he couldn't remove the elaborate war mask. The whole scheme depended on it. Only thus could the myth that had become Ajatashatru be played out.

Mara took in the ripple of muscle beneath the leather torso plate of the charging warrior. Suddenly a patch of cloud passed overhead and from the shadow resolved features, sharp cheekbones and jowl. Freshly-oiled hair, a vermillion smear on his forehead, the mark of his protecting deity now faded by sun and sweat.

Another youth trying to live and die by the warrior's code. Both of us followers of the same code, oath-bound to different masters and different causes. Was anyone right or were both wrong?

He could smell the fresh earth and grass dislodged by the racing wheels. The sun started to bristle the hair on the back of his neck. The enemy's face staring into Mara's, was a palette of piercing hatred and grim resolve, fear and courage, agony and rapture. The bowstring was pulled hard against the man's lips, twisting them into a dreadful smile.

Poor, poor man. He thinks he's going to kill a king today.

Ah, my friend, how we both, fundamentally flawed, lie between light and dark, understanding and committing to neither. Our display of fear or strength is unwitting and unwilling. And our destinies, intertwined.

Mara felt deep regret at the waste.

Please stop! Turn back! Don't die! Not by my arrows.

He closed his eyes. For a moment he contemplated staying that way. He could feel the tremor begin in his right arm. It was not a tic or a twitch, but something deep in his sinews and bones or even beyond. He didn't know. He knew that this had started happening recently each time he went into battle. His arm would become heavy and strangely non-cooperative each time he had to wield the heavy bow. It took a huge effort for the warrior to take over. He opened his eyes and drew an arrow.

The charioteer and he were the perfect team. At the last moment, his driver turned their chariot sideways, changing the angle to the oncoming enemy. The side was reinforced by tall interlocking shields set like fish scales. Mara leant into the protective nook. No arrow could penetrate that.

It followed like poetry.

The enemy fired his arrow from just twenty yards. It came whistling through the air, but thudded harmlessly into the heavy shields.

Mara pulled out an arrow from his quiver. Each one was a work of art. Two feet long, balanced by goose feathers painted crimson and tipped by a handspan of razor-sharp iron. They were made for a king.

'Live forever!' Mara whispered as he shot. It was the warrior's prayer for an adversary, for those about to die.

It flew from his bow with a hum, its feathers making it spin and accelerate. It hit the enemy high in the chest and went through the leather and bronze armour without check. It spun the young warrior around and transfixed him to the side of his chariot. He was dead before his open mouth could form a cry.

Draw – shoot – pray – kill. Minimum effort, maximum effect.

Just like it said in the shastras, the code of the warrior.

His arm was trembling and he was bathed in sweat. He knew that his men were watching, but it was beyond him to control it.

The squadrons of chariots fanned out behind him, dust swirling from the wheels and coloured pennants dancing in the wind.

The air reverberated with the victory cries of his men. 'Ajatashatru! Ajatashatru!'

He raised his hand, palm outward, just like the emperor. He felt disgusted at what he had to do. This was Ajatashatru's formula to deal with any revolt. And he was but Ajatashatru's shadow. He looked at the leader of the revolution who had been brought before him in chains. He took a deep breath and readied himself to be the emperor.

'Let it be known before these vultures you call your men, before your women and hirelings, that we have crushed your evil,' he clicked his fingers, 'Just like that. This is the power of Magadha. The power you attempted to challenge.'

He ordered five hundred men to be impaled on stakes. The ringleaders were roped to the back of chariots and dragged to Rajgriha. By the time they reached, the ropes dragged just bloody smears.

'I don't necessarily enjoy this, Mara,' the emperor had once told him, 'but power is amoral and if not exerted outward, it singes everything inside. We must quell all raised voices. Magadha can never be a superpower without an assured supply of their copper and iron. It is no different with any nation striving for greatness. It was always so and so it always will be.'

Mara's life till now had been a blessing. Being born into a family of kshatriyas was a privilege in a land where caste was everything. He was a natural archer and charioteer and had carved out quite a reputation for himself. None of these, however, matched his other natural talent. He resembled Ajatashatru. Not just in height and build, but down to the hooked nose and the cleft in the chin. The emperor used him as his double. Decked in Ajatashatru's mask and armour, he would appear in places the emperor could not be in. It was known that one of the seven miracles that the devas could perform was the ability to be in many places at the same time. Ajatashatru became a god. So clever was the subterfuge that even his own men were fooled.

At forty years of age, he had everything a man could want. Wealth, glory, a lovely wife, a sixteen-year-old boy itching to follow in his footsteps, and the respect of his peers.

This rampant killing would never stop. I have traded riches and rank for blood!

Nonsense! Even thinking this way is weakness. There is nothing wrong with what I do. Every man is born to do his dharma, his sworn duty. That defines his place in society. It is my dharma to serve the emperor and protect the land. Not only is Ajatashatru emperor, he is also a living god. What is wrong in serving a god?

Ha! Serve your god if you can. He's as fearsome as he's magnanimous. Let's see how he treats hunting hounds who've lost their fangs. Ajatashatru would see your confusion as dissidence. You would be stripped of everything. The emperor is god only to those in his favour. If power can corrupt, what does divine power do? Corrupt divinely?

Mara struggled to smother this jabbering dialogue in his head.

He was finished, he could sense that. He'd never be able to wield his bow again. Never kill again. He felt lost.

Ajatashatru would never let him go. He was a vital cog in the emperor's machine. Without him, Ajatashatru was a mere mortal. With him, he was divine – a myth, a phantom.

Where on earth was he planning to go, anyway?

If not steel, what else could he depend upon? If not war, what was his profession? If not the emperor, who else could he serve? He remembered many a battle fought with him on one side of the field and Ajatashatru on the other. Enemies, each more deadlier than the other, swarmed around them. They had stood in their chariots proud and awesome, and had faced faced the awful rain of arrows so fierce that the very clouds seemed to vomit death. And each time they'd come out winners.

Maybe this mysterious ailment was just plain fear. Naked, debilitating fear that overwhelms you just before battle, when you want to run and save your body from being shredded by blade or lance. When you don't care about anything or anyone, just your own survival. He wished it was that simple.

Courage never comes naturally to any man. Human flesh always flinches at the sight of cold steel. The best any warrior can do is manage his fears well. Never mind the poetry and ballads, the ode to valour. Those were for bards to make a living. As a young man he had tried everything – intense yoga, painful austerities, even fumes of poppy. Fear was as familiar as an old mistress. He knew its guile. He'd learned to subdue and manipulate it. One could trick the body to not feel fear, but what about the soul?

The city glowed like the hive of a million fireflies. The festival of lamps was the most auspicious day in the Hindu calendar. Rajgriha, the capital of Ajatashatru's empire was decked with floral arches and coloured banners. Heaps of sandalwood and aloe perfumed the air. Like a bride alighting from the palanquin, like his Lata the day she first stepped into his home, his land and his woman both looked desirous and vulnerable. And he'd sworn to protect both.

The high point of the festival was the emperor's parade. Mara, as a winner of the gold talon of praise, was given a place of honour. He loved being in his freshly polished armour, mounted on his chestnut charger, both doffed and eager.

Ajatashatru himself led the parade in a squadron of chariots. Sixteen black horses pulled his chariot. Their hides glowed and strips of white silk were plaited into their manes. The entire assembly of nobles was present. The Aryan race was known for its good looks. The tight-fitting, burnished breast plates and brocaded capes showed off each lean, broad-shouldered physique to perfection.

Ajatashatru, the leader of the nation, stood tall and proud, clad in gold armour and a ceremonial mask. The light reflecting off the butter-yellow metal framed him in a halo. He looked like Surya,the sun god himself..

The ceremonies began. Mara was led up to the emperor. He was to be felicitated for his long service. Trumpets sounded. It was a heady moment. He saw his wife Lata in the crowd. Suddenly he was pinned down by the guards. The gold talon was torn from his neck. His face was blackened with soaked charcoal – the ultimate public disgrace, reserved for deserters and traitors. His right arm was paralyzed, he couldn't stop them. His body was slick with sweat.

He came out of his sleep, screaming. It was a recurring nightmare.

The boy's eyes flashed with a mix of anger and disbelief. The expression was so familiar. Did he get it from Lata? No, it was even closer. Mara felt he was looking at himself. The look he'd get when he thought an injustice was being done. He'd just told his son not to join the Imperial Service.

It's unfair, he's been preparing for this his whole life. Service to the empire and personal glory are the reasons for a warrior's existence. Teach this long enough to malleable minds and they believe it.

The boy was ready. A body honed by gruelling training and a mind tempered by the tradition of the warriors. Only his upbringing restrained the boy from shouting at his father.

You're cheating him of his inheritance. Isn't it natural for a son to step into his father's shoes?

Was he getting ready then, to vacate his shoes?

Lata rushed to their son's side.

'Surely you joke about this, my lord?'

She always used the respectful title when angry.

'We know you are suffering from something. Maybe it's fatigue or a touch of nerves. You don't even know yourself, but whatever it is, it'll pass. You can't ruin our son's future and ours because of something like that.'

He should have known that he'd have to face Lata.

Lata, his beautiful wife of eighteen years. She was gracious and kind, talented and aware. And blessed with a burning ambition. She'd always hidden it well from others. When they were to be married, Mara was the brightest star in the emperor's army, with a glorious future ahead of him, and that's why her family had chosen him. They had sent him a dowry large enough to raise his rank to theirs. She possessed jewels and silks finer than his superiors' wives, but was careful never to wear them publicly, lest she ruffle any feathers. She'd always pressed him to do better, be smarter, and do whatever it took to make it to the top. Even the rank he held now as master of hundred chariots was because of her constant pushing.

'You are the best warrior in the land. Everyone says so. You should be master of the entire chariot regiment, if not the commander of the imperial armies. You have to be like a peacock, my dear, and strut around with your feathers puffed, reminding others of your accomplishments.'

Wives harbour ambitions far greater than their men. Emperor Ajatashatru would do well to recruit them in the front ranks, he thought.

He had gone as far as his skill could take him. To rise beyond this, more cunning and politicking were required.

Lata would let her disappointment show as she watched their son growing up. Mara knew that she had transferred her hopes to him.

'He has the blood of warriors in him. He'll make a great one himself. They've already offered to make him an officer.'

'All this talk of blood and lineage and code is nonsense. Empty words. Nobody knows what they mean. Men just follow each other so as not to look bad in front of other fellows.' Mara had wanted to say these words for so long.

Lata was shocked.

'I can't believe you said that. People live and die by that code. Once you take an oath, you stake your life on it! Does your honour mean nothing to you?'

'Fighting sticks' was a game the children of warriors played. They were taught swordplay, but they parried with sticks instead of swords. Mara remembered when his son had been sent back home in shame one day for breaking another boy's nose.

Everybody admonished my son, but I had patted him on the back secretly for playing well and winning at all cost. We create a world and its rules for our children to inherit. Can we blame them if they turn out to be monsters?

'He'll suffer!' Mara cried out. 'I want to prevent that. I don't want him to reach the state that I have – paralyzed by his mind, confused about all that you speak about ... duty, loyalty and false oaths.'

'These values you criticize have given you everything, and today you would deny that to your own son!'

He remembered the vedic ceremony. As a young father, he had selected the ingredients for his son's first food according to the qualities he wanted his son to have. Rice with melted butter so that he may attain glory, ram's meat for physical strength, and honey for loyalty. He had created the menu and here he was now, cursing the preparation.

'Look at him! He's young and capable. He can't help it. He's got your blood in his veins, after all. He's raring for a chance to prove himself in combat.'

Mara sighed. 'No great dependence should be placed on

the eagerness of young minds for action. Let me tell you, war is attractive only to those who are strangers to it.'

She was looking into his eyes. He knew that his deep-set brown eyes had developed dark patches under them. Once she had called his eyes smouldering.

Then, mind you, don't get burnt.

Suddenly there were tears in her eyes.

'I won't allow this madness to destroy our son's future. There are others who will help your son, if you don't. And if you try and stop him, Mara ... I will take him and go away!'

They'd got to her. How did he think he could be bigger than the lure of the system?

Hindu wives never addressed their husbands by name. He must have really slipped down the scale.

The following week, Mara's son took the royal oath and joined the Imperial Service.

In the age-old ritual, with a mark of the sacred vermillion on his forehead, and a sprinkling of holy water, his son was ushered into manhood. It was a joyous occasion. Mara could feel nothing but despair.

In his son's face he could see his own and his father's and his ancestors', all morphed into one entity, parading in tow to lay themselves at an altar. He could hear the blare of conch shells and kettle drums, hoof beats and battle cries, clashing of metal, grunting of curses, and mortal fear, the bodies maimed and dead, of both friend and foe. The wine-drenched recounting of battles, the temporary relief of taverns and whores. Bodies deeply scarred and souls deliberately numbed. The life of a warrior!

Even before the last of the rituals was complete, the first speech makers were on their feet. There was a vast collection of sycophantic and patriotic clichés waiting to be mouthed.

His turn came last. He could not contain himself. Teary-eyed, he began to recount the burden of killing and bloodshed that no holy water or imperial sanction could wash away.

In this gathering of distinguished warriors, his words were sacrilege. His friends led him away before he could do more damage.

The commander of the army confronted him. He was a tall grey beard with a typically erect military posture. His breast plates gleamed from years of valet care.

The kind tones did not cloak the dire threat.

'Mara, there is only so much that people will tolerate from their colleagues, especially from the more successful ones. Maybe you've had enough. Maybe you should have retired. Whatever your choice, you should have gone quietly. This is indecent, it's almost treason, and there are those who want to have you incarcerated. Frankly, after this, I won't be able to hold off the dogs. I don't know what ails you my friend, but it is best that you take this disease elsewhere before Ajatashatru hears about it. Leave the country now or even I can't save you.'

He isn't worried for me, he's only scared the rot might spread.

He saw his wife and son retreat into the shadow of one of the great pillars of the hall. When he looked again, they were gone.

Lata, my love, are you scared of being infected too?

On a grey overcast day, Mara left his home and his life of forty years. Was it only Ajatashatru's need to keep their history secret that allowed him to leave? He'd heard a rumour that the emperor hadn't been keeping well. For the first time, Ajatashatru had cancelled all campaigns and called his armies back.

Clad only in a robe and sandals, Mara went, facing the world for the first time without chariot or bow. He felt naked. He didn't know what he was looking for except it was imperative to find it. His military mind revolted at the lack of direction and objective.

How does one seek without knowing what is to be sought?

For many weeks he drifted, preferring to say that he was in exile rather than lost. Better a political entity than an aimless wanderer. Then he fell in with a group of bards who sang hymns about the lure of the 'wide open road' and the romantic, perfect state of 'homelessness'. Music and the fumes of a hashish chillum in lieu of a home. Some wealthy traders honoured them as 'bhikkus' (almsmen) and became their patrons. He felt like an imposter. The warrior clans had regarded most of these renunciants as feeble dropouts. This was no cure for his restlessness. He left them.

The times, it seemed, were aflame with the spirit of enquiry and quest. Dozens of cults had sprung up, catering to varied appetites. He joined one which propagated midnight marches with whirling torches and drums, robes of severe yellow and frequent daubing of the forehead with ash. After many miles with them, he had found nothing but a severe itching of his forehead.

He fled northward to the Himalayas and discovered a mountainscape fed by streams from pristine glaciers. Amidst enchanting forests of chinar and shisham, and meadows of balsam, he sought peace. But nothing.

He lived for months with a hermit who prescribed a regime of self-deprivation. Days of starvation and hours of lying immersed in an ice-water lake in the hope of 'expanding his mind'. He became sick and wandered in and out of delirium for days. All that expanded was his knowledge of pain. If he hadn't left, he would have died.

Would this quest never to end?

He didn't know for how long he travelled or where he went or when he crossed the border and entered the kingdom of Ajatashatru again. When he came out of his stupor, he found himself alongside many others who were trudging along a dusty path close to the capital Rajgriha. A long winding row of humanity slowly ascended the slopes of a hill. Each time he felt weak, someone offered an arm or a shoulder to help. A dark-hooked, beak-like rock gave the hill its name, Eagle's Peak. Those coming downhill spoke in hushed tones.

'Your worries will be over. He will lift your burden. He will show you the way.'

'Buddham sharanam! Buddham sharanam!' It went on and on like a chant.

Who are they talking about? Who's 'he'? Another holy man? Huh, I've seen many ... They're all experts at kind smiles and quoting useless scriptures.

They came to a bamboo grove. Hundreds sat cross-legged on the ground, mesmerized by a figure amidst them. The light of the setting sun took on the quality of water. It seemed to pour, wash, splash and soak the entire gathering. Curiously, it seemed to emanate more from the figure than the sun.

The atmosphere, he couldn't put it in words, a cool serenity that delighted at its own existence.

The figure was clad in a saffron robe. He seemed to be looking at Mara and speaking directly to him. Mara was too far to hear the words, but his voice was like the sounds of nature itself, deep, resonating ... comforting.

For the first time in months, Mara began to feel relieved.

Am I home?

The people listened, rapt. The words were undramatic, with neither rhetoric nor a deliberate appeal to emotion. There was such promise in his words that many wept.

As he went closer, he saw the face of the man. It was that of someone very familiar, a friend or a relative. No, even closer. Mara felt he was looking at a mirror, a perfect version of himself. A best that he'd never dreamt he could be.

He folded his hands.

'Help me, I'm lost,' he wailed. 'I've killed and maimed hundreds in my life in the call of duty.' Mara was crying openly.

If he expected his tears to be wiped away, he was mistaken. The man's voice was kindly, but stern, like a teacher's.

'Tears are a product of your emotions. And emotion is the wrong key to sort out right and wrong. So rid yourself of tears and exhausting emotions. If you're feeling sorry for having taken so many lives, don't. Because life can never be created or destroyed by anyone. It only changes shape and form. If anything, you should feel sorry for yourself. Each time you've killed, the only thing you've destroyed is your own compassion. And compassion is the essence of every life. It's the best you can be. So the feeling of being lost comes when you go against the best you can be.'

'I feel so ... guilty,' Mara said.

'Don't. Guilt is the most useless of all emotions. If you've created hell by your actions, guilt will not let you walk away or reform. It is like hell revisited.

'For now, understand that it is enough to kill the will to kill. Start with that. You'll be surprised at the kind of solutions you can come up with if you take away killing as an option. Remember this: first take away killing as an option. People often say that killing is their last resort. But when pressed by greed or glory, their last resort often becomes the first response.

'When you were young, you must have thought your happiness would endure for ever. But unless happiness has a firm foundation in faith and right causes, your life can change to a very unhappy one without your being aware of it. The same is true for a community or even a nation. Building empires without building a conscience will lead to certain collapse.

'All of us have the potential to discover that conscience. But while bringing it out in you, there will be conflict with your old villains and champions. With your wishes, fears, dreams, hopes and triumphs. The experience will make you excited, depressed, angry, afraid, joyous, but ultimately … free.'

Mara's mind suddenly started unfolding in layers, bringing back each horrible image of violence from the past. Each locked up emotion connected to these images seemed to have washed away.

The chattering voice which seemed to be at odds with him all the time seemed to extinguish. He felt free to find a single voice again.

'But what can I do? What can one man do in this world? I'm but a shadow.'

'One man can change the destiny of millions. It's always been that way. Even a shadow can influence its master.'

Mara's body started trembling and tears streamed freely down his face. He fell at the feet of the man.

'Tell me, who are you? Are you a god?'

The man smiled.

'No, I'm not.'

'Are you an angel or a sage?'

'No, I'm just a man like you and you can become exactly like me.'

'Who are you?'

'I'm awake.'

Mara staggered away. There were others in queue, eager to ease their suffering.

Take away killing as an option? Could the truth really be that simple?

He saw the other faces around him, burdened by worry and doubt. One face seemed very familiar and very out-of-place. Mara was stunned.

Sitting in the front row, devoid of any trappings of royalty, deep furrows of anguish and confusion on his face, was Ajatashatru. Ajatashatru, in whose name they wrote the law, at whose bidding he had killed scores.

Not an emperor or a venerated god anymore, just a man like everyone else. A trapped soul seeking refuge.

Even a shadow can influence its master, he had said.

Project Ha Ha

The Mosquito aircraft was like a slingshot launched from England towards the heart of Nazi Germany. Its official name was the Mosquito–S. Pilots who flew it liked to assume the S stood for slingshot. Actually, on record, S simply meant 'special version'.

This airplane flew alone and was immune to the dangers of the wartime night skies. The anti-aircraft guns and night fighters could not reach it, that's how high it flew. Even the radar beams could not track it properly because it was made of wood. This one tonight was angling towards Bremen, leading his flock of a hundred heavy bombers to lay waste one of the centres of German wartime industry.

He was the 'pathfinder' and was equipped with special, newly invented electronic gear to find the target at night. The thing was that this new marvel worked only at a height of thirty thousand feet. To get to thirty thousand feet, the Mosquito had been made lighter by stripping it of almost everything, including its guns. In recognition of its ability to see in the dark, the Mosquito was code-named 'Vampire'.

Once the Mosquito found Bremen, he would lay his brightly burning, multi-coloured markers on it. All that the heavy Lancaster bombers following him had to do was look for these 'Christmas tree' coloured lights and drop their bomb load.

It was 1942. The plan, worked out by the brightest brains of the Royal Air Force, was going well. Each night raid into Germany was leaving 'the Nazis yelping', as reported by the British dailies.

Flying Officer Alan McCartney and Flight Sergeant Peter Hill sat side by side in the cramped cockpit of the Mosquito. The moonlight had transformed the upper sky into a floodlit arena. The plane sped along, its dark shadow being flicked from cloud to cloud far below.

Bremen was still ten minutes away.

'Like dancing naked in the moonlight, eh?' Alan said.

'And no one to see us. Shame, innit?' Peter smiled.

'The heavies must be in that muck,' Alan said, pointing to the thick cloud below.

'I pity these bomber lads. Dunno what I'd hate more, getting tossed around and flyin' blind in a cloud or being butt naked in full view of every anti-aircraft gun. Thank all the saints we're up here. Ours is a good job!'

'Ours is a sensible job,' Alan said.

'Not very sporting though, is it? I mean, to be up here where no one can get you.'

'There's nothing sporting about getting killed, my friend.'

The clouds below them parted briefly and they could see their own heavy bombers below them. Puffy cotton balls filled the sky around the bombers. The German flak had got their range. Suddenly a dozen pinpricks of brilliant light appeared over one of the bombers. One of its wings was in flames.

'Oh, shit! Look at that! She's hit! She's going!' Peter yelled. They watched as the first parachute came out, then another. Three, four, five, six floated away. Then the stricken bomber slowly rolled over.

Alan's mouth was dry. Six parachutes, it was always like that. The pilot never got out, he had to hold the plane steady while the others jumped. By the time it was his turn, the centrifugal force would have pinned him to the seat.

'Fallen friends,' Peter said suddenly. He was making the traditional toast to lost comrades.

'Fallen friends,' Alan whispered, feeling guilty that they'd never had to raise a glass to a dead squadron mate. They hadn't lost a single 'Vampire' yet.

'Thank you, lord, for this beauty,' Alan whispered, gripping the control column tightly. Thank god, the flak couldn't touch them at this altitude.

Earlier that day, the two of them had been out for brunch to celebrate Alan's twenty-first birthday. Only in wartime could a true-blue aristocrat and a cockney lad from London's East End share the confines of a fighter plane and a table at a fancy restaurant with girls from the secretary pool. Nothing like facing the constant threat of a fiery death together to dispense with class barriers.

Peter's wide, friendly mouth was pursed in a whistle, the opening bars of '*Tiger rag*'.

This was the cue for Alan to speak.

'Ours really is the cushiest job of the war. We fly at night, out of sight and out of reach ... of everybody. We're back for breakfast. Sleep in the best billets in the mess, which are reserved for us, a game of tennis in the evening, then off again three times a week.'

These girls had never been out with fliers. But after three years of war they were used to men of different uniforms bragging about their heroics. Alan and Peter had realized that the reverse approach worked better.

Peter's cockney nicely offset Alan's upper-class diction.

'Luv the way you speak, guv. He can make the bleedin' mess menu sound like Shakespeare. It's not all a breeze, girls, these long hops are a killer for the bladder. He never mentions the tin can we carry on the long flight.'

'Right, or the fact that you carry and use two!' Alan quipped.

'Anyway, we have all the time in the world to take you ladies to the Milroy in London for the weekend, is what my mate is tryin' to tell you. Innit, Alan?' Peter asked between mouthfuls of herrings and onions. Alan had warned him about the ill effects of this stuff incase they got close to the girls later, but he just wouldn't listen.

Alan leant back in his chair to light a cigarette and looked at the dark-haired girl sitting opposite him.

'Don't get involved' had been his advice to Peter, regardless of who the girl was that they went out with. For Peter, in spite of his tough East Ender exterior, tended towards mush in these matters. What Alan couldn't understand was his own reaction to Victoria. He had always had the fast talk and looks to attract women. But she made him feel as gawky as a teenager. Unlike the other girls in the typists' pool, she had a public school education and real class. She'd been steadily warding off his advances and suddenly he wanted to bend his own rule of non-involvement just this once.

The huge German Freya radar antenna swung with slow deliberation. Like the goddess it was named after, it could see in the dark for a hundred miles all around.

In the dimly lit air defence centre, a controller raised a hand. 'First contact, sir.'

And so the night battle began, the players from both sides groping at each other like knife fighters wearing blindfolds.

The German officer on duty was a natural. A radar intercept officer's job required a powerful instinct and Colonel Fischer's were honed like a hound. He knew the pathfinder Mosquito was just minutes ahead of the bomber stream. To get him was to make the rest blind.

The timing had to be just right. Tonight he judged it to perfection.

'Wait for it,' he said, watching the blips slide across the radar screen. 'Wait ... Now!'

That was the signal to launch Vulture, the specialty on tonight's menu.

'See anyone else?' Alan asked. Peter swivelled his head to do a cursory sweep. 'Nothin', boss.'

'Your biggest enemy is solitude, boys,' their squadron commander used to say before every trip.

'Twenty more of these flights and we're through. End of tour, push papers in the command office and shiny new medals apiece. You'll look dapper in a gong, guv.' Peter grinned.

Alan sighed. 'Yup, girls love medals, my friend.'

Bremen was just five minutes away.

'Arm the marker bombs,' Alan told Peter.

Often they did their entire mission without a glimpse of any other aircraft.

But tonight they were not alone.

A specially equipped German Junkers-88 night fighter was tailing them. It had a newly developed supercharger that could take it up to these altitudes that the Mosquitoes thought only they inhabited. Its call sign was Vulture.

Fischer sipped his coffee without tasting it. He watched the two blips on the radar screen representing his night fighter and the bomber stream rushing towards each other at a combined speed of six hundred miles per hour. He couldn't see the Mosquito but he knew it would be there, just ahead of the bombers. He waited till the blips almost overlapped.

'Vulture, now!' Fischer ordered.

In the Junkers, pilot Lieutenant Brandt yanked back the control stick and rammed open the supercharger. Teetering on the edge of a stall, the German plane was kicked up another eight thousand feet and spotted the Mosquito almost immediately.

The squadron's anniversary party would be in full swing. The old room would be smelling of roast duck, schnapps and cigars. Smells that seeped into the oak panelling and joined memories of other dinners in happier times. To miss out on that fare after three years of wartime rationing, was terrible luck.

'Can't be spared, Brandt. Only you hotshots can fly the secret plane,' his commanding officer had told him. Brandt detected the envy. Even the CO had not been trained to fly the special planes. Only those with superb reflexes and sharp night vision had been chosen. Only the very young possessed both those qualities. Brandt was turning twenty that year.

He'd missed the party tonight. The girls from the nursing centre would be there. Last time, he'd mustered his guts and asked one for a dance. She would be there again. He panicked for a moment: would one of his mates try to charm her? The sight of the Mosquito in his gun sight calmed him again; it made up for everything.

No matter how sophisticated the weapons, warrior vocabulary has always been primitive. Brandt reported his sighting of the target to Fischer at the radar centre with the words, 'Iron Cross! Iron Cross!' He parroted the words, not knowing that they dated back to the Middle Ages. It was the traditional cry of the vampire killer, in the act of killing.

There was a sudden roaring sound followed by a thump that jarred their spines. The controls were wrenched from Alan's hands. The windscreen was smashed and glass from the instrument panel billowed out in a cloud. The engines screamed a couple of octaves higher.

Out of control, the Mosquito dived sharply. Only then did they see their predator, its wings shining in the moonlight as it turned to find them for a second attack. The Mosquito had no guns to fight back with. The designers had kept it as light as possible to fly higher. Alan tried to dive towards the banks of cloud to hide in. But like a dark wolf pelting downhill, the matt black Junkers dove towards them. They saw pinpricks of lights on its nose and in a steady hose, flaming ball-like objects slammed into their wooden wings.

'Christ! She's falling apart!' Peter yelled.

'Jettison the bombs.' Alan wanted to make them lighter.

Alan saw lines of flaming shells coming at them and all he could think of was what Victoria had told him when he'd taken her aside to kiss her.

She'd pushed him firmly away and said, 'It's Peter.'

And he'd understood in a flash why she'd been avoiding him all this while – because of Peter. Peter, his friend and co-pilot. Peter, of the broad features and rough accent. Uncomplicated and unschooled Peter.

'Why Peter?' he'd blurted out.

'I don't know. There's something so honest about him. I've never met someone so guileless, so easy in his skin. No man has made me feel this way before. Almost ... I don't know ... gawky.'

Alan smiled. He knew the feeling. He should have seen it before. It was only his belief in his infallibility with women that had blinded him.

'It's going, boss!' Peter's yell brought him back.

Alan smiled grimly, 'Okay, bail out. Quickly. I have to hold her or neither of us will get out.'

The left engine was now coughing blue flame and spitting orange sparks. He saw Peter hesitate.

'Get out or I'm going to jump and leave the plane to you! Get out ... GO!'

Peter climbed out then and was plucked away by the air stream. Alan saw the white canopy of his parachute far below. They were still over land, he might be made prisoner, but at least he'd be safe, he thought.

Brandt looked up and could see every detail of the Mosquito. The two planes roared through the sky until, judging the moment well, Brandt pulled back the control stick. The Junkers' nose seemed to touch the Mosquito's belly. He pressed the gun button and raked it from nose to tail. The two twenty mm cannons fitted in the Junkers' nose fired at a rate of 520 rounds per minute. In the first burst, he held the button down for only five seconds and in that hellish instant, ninety shells raced towards the Mosquito. Thirty struck the plane. Any more than twenty hits were considered lethal. He turned back for a second run and did it again.

A red light was on in the cockpit. He'd had his half hour of fun and now the supercharger was spent. He turned away from the stricken Mosquito. It was finished anyway. Brandt wondered if the high command would let him add it to his tally. They were so damn keen to keep the special supercharger secret. He wondered if the party was still on. And would she still be there?

The first sharp pang had settled into a dull wet ache. Shrapnel from the first explosion had entered his back. Life had drained out of his lower limbs. Alan realized that there was no way he could have climbed out of the cockpit, though his first instinct had been to jump and leave Peter. Had he changed his mind because he couldn't, or was this the first truly selfless act of his life? What the hell! He felt too drained to work it out. At least one of them would make it back to Victoria. The one she wanted.

The plane, of its own accord, had stopped its wild dive and was descending in wide circles and heading out to sea. The Mosquito met the waves in a grey splash and was sucked under. A couple of minutes later, Peter floated down smoothly into a ploughed field. He saw a farmhouse in flames. People were trying to douse the fire with buckets of water. They saw him in the light of the flames and ran out to him.

Damn! It's too late to make a run for it, he thought.

He fumbled for his revolver, then stopped. These were simple folk, a lot like his own. He didn't want to harm them.

He greeted them with his friendly grin. The men surrounded him. They killed him with their spades. It was a bright red-coloured marker bomb from a British plane that had destroyed their farm.

Small terraced houses and dark chimneys formed the backdrop to the newly made whitewashed huts and corrugated rooftops. Bletchely was the home of British counter-intelligence. A small town on the track from Cambridge now held more secrets than the Tower of London ever had.

The air marshal's leathery face was immobile as he paced the room. His anxiety was infectious. He'd passed his pack of cigarettes around and they'd all lit up. Napoleon, he'd read, had used this simple device to become popular with his fellows. He squinted through the fog of tobacco, rheumy eyes examining the counter-intelligence team.

'So, gentlemen, the air force is not getting itself in a twist over the loss of a few planes. But in the last few nights we've lost every special Mosquito we sent. If the Mosquitoes can't lead the bombers to the target, frankly, that's the end of a meaningful bombing campaign. Churchill is using every trick to convince the Yanks to send their air force over. But if the Yanks figure out that we're doubtful of our own bombing, they're not going to jump in. And without them, honestly, who knows about the war.'

He let that sink in. A lot of people assumed that after the Battle of Britain, the Royal Air Force was unbeatable. Fact was, Britain was running short of planes and pilots. Way too short.

'This is straight from the PM. Top priority. Find out how the Germans are doing it. Lock yourselves up in this hut, day and night, if you have to. They're not supposed to have anything that can fly that high. Your own report says that, dammit!' He slammed the manila folder on the table.

Hut Eight got into action: decoding German air force signals, activating agents embedded deep in German industry and government. Examine every angle, check every theory, was their brief.

Finally Jerico was brought up.

'Many years ago, we recruited an agent in Germany. He's risen to be quite high up in their air force high command. Close to their chief, Goering himself. His code name is Jerico. We were saving him for something big.'

Nothing was bigger. Activate Jerico was the order.

Wilheim Stoller's importance lay in the fact that he was Rita Stoller's kid brother. Rita Stoller was a leading German actress and a model. She was also Reich Marshal Goering's mistress.

'Take care of little Willy, darling. He has always been a bit of a loser.'

Goering didn't mind Willy at all. He was rather fond of his harmless, eager-to-please personality. Goering was the supreme commander of the air force. He'd given Willy work at the Air Force headquarters as a clerk. Willy had done surprisingly well and risen to become a senior aide. He'd proven himself to be a good employee and a dedicated Nazi.

Goering would have been shocked to learn that years ago, little Willy had been a card carrying member of the communist party and an activist at many 'red' rallies.

When the Nazis came to power, a massive witch hunt had been launched to wipe out the 'commies'.

Willy had set fire to his local party records and successfully gone underground. One evening, after a couple of cognacs, he'd told Goering, 'My best friend believes that no matter which war it is or who wins or loses, the ultimate price of any war is paid by the working class.'

'What!' Goering roared. 'Your friend is a bloody Red. No patriot speaks that way. He should be shot dead.'

'He was, sir, last week in North Africa. They gave him the Knight's Cross, for exceptional bravery.'

'I know what the Knight's Cross is for,' Goering said impatiently. 'Life is about allegiance, Willy. Every man should know where his allegiance lies.'

Wilheim Stoller realized then and there where his lay. He threw in his lot with what he considered the bastion of the working classes – Russia.

He allowed himself to be recruited by the KGB and fed them important information from time to time. His Russian masters ran him under the code name krolik, rabbit in Russian. Then, as it often happens in the murky world of international espionage, they traded their pet krolik in return for a favour from the British. Not that Willy ever knew. He still reported to the Russians and via them to the British. Unknown to him, his British keepers had given him a new name – Jerico.

It took a while, but gradually the information started trickling in. The Nazis had got something all right. It was top secret. They were calling it the 'pathfinder killer'. Jerico, alias Krolik, fighting as he believed for world communism, had delivered. 'Harlein Harlein' were the words spoken in hushed tones that were instantly picked up at German air force headquarters.

It was the brainchild of a certain Dr Otto Kesller. Painstakingly, they put together all there was to know about him, from kindergarten down to the last filling in his teeth. 'Harlein' leapt out of their report. It was a comedy club in Hamburg for which Dr Otto wrote skits in his spare time. Why the hell would a top German scientist name his ultra-secret project after a comedy club?

The counter-intelligence team was a group of men of varied talents: mathematicians, linguists, scientists, crossword puzzle champions and even a stand-up comic. It took them seventy-two sleepless hours to crack it. The breakthrough came from the comedy artist. The first letters of 'Harlein Harlein' were Ha Ha. The Germans had not named the project on a whim. It was a code for nitrous oxide, commonly called laughing gas.

Dr Otto had discovered that nitrous oxide, when injected into an aircraft engine could boost its performance by twenty-five per cent.

'That bloody simple, huh!' the air marshal kept repeating. He reached for the phone and was connected to the air force's engineering department.

The chief of the team was the crossword puzzle champion.

'There's another thing, sir. They call these planes

Vultures. You see, they know we call ours Vampires.' He flicked ash untidily around the ashtray.

'There is a story from medieval times, part of the Dracula lore actually. When vampires preyed on a village, the villagers would generally abandon their homes. Vampires were invincible except when it came to the claws of a vulture. Only a vulture knew the way to kill a vampire. So the villagers got themselves a vulture.'

The air marshall nodded, fascinated.

'We're giving teeth back to our vampires. I've asked them to fit guns on our Mosquitoes. Soon they'll be killing these bloody vultures.'

'In the story, the struggle between the vampires and vultures goes on forever.'

There was an ominous silence. Then one of the teammates cleared his throat.

'I hope this damn Ha Ha report is worth it, sir. We heard that Jerico was picked up last night by the Gestapo.'

There was silence again. They all knew that sleeper agents were good for one mission alone. That was their shelf life.

To Dr Otto Keslller, machinery held a strange fascination. It was like something feminine to his masculinity, like engaging with the wiles and vagaries of a woman. A ladies' man, he treated all engines the way he treated his women. He could plead, beg, rant, fight, lie and cheat to win them over. But most of all, he prized his skill as a 'humourist' to get the best out of them. Nothing like a bawdy joke or limerick to turn an engine or lady over, he'd often say. Humour developed patience and fortitude, good Saxon virtues both, he believed.

Ever since he'd started writing skits for the Harlein Club, his life had changed. He was being invited to parties in places and with people he'd only heard of. Years of tinkering with engines and being a distinguished scientist had never rewarded him this way. So when the chief of the air force had asked what he would like to name his new invention, he had the name ready.

'The Ha Ha project, Herr Reich Marshal.'

Goering stared at him for a moment, then threw back his head and laughed.

'Nothing more invigorating than a bit of humour in wartime, eh, Otto?'

'Especially in wartime, Herr Reich Marshal.'

'Project Ha Ha! That's a good one.' Goering leant closer. It was the end of a long party and the Reich marshal had downed a few.

'After the war, Otto, you'll have a great future entertaining the rich fat cats in Berlin and Hamburg.'

He turned to leave and Otto came to attention. I wonder, Reich Marshal, if it is the German cities where the people will be rich and fat after the war. But Otto kept this wisecrack to himself. The Reich marshal would not have seen the humour in it.

Otto knew the old tale about the vulture and the vampire. He knew that the success of any project was temporary. And in the constantly shifting fortunes of this war, nobody knew who would have the last laugh.

'Putra'

PROLOGUE

Dr Naval Kishore Srivastava is a high-profile lawyer practicing in the Supreme Court. He lives with his wife Shruti in Delhi. They are middle-aged and do not have any children.

Naval is known as a brilliant lawyer with a flair for revolutionary theories in his field, which is criminal law. His client list reads like a veritable who's who of the underworld and their inevitable kin, the politicians. Of late, however, he has been criticized for his methods. It is felt that he puts too much emphasis on the workings of the criminal mind. He treats all critics, both within the legal community and outside it, with complete disdain.

With the upcoming general elections, it seems that a new party may be coming to power. And Naval, as a loyalist of this party, is tipped to be the next Attorney General. This is a great ride for Naval's mammoth ego. It is a just reward, he feels, for his brilliance.

He finds it difficult to contain his euphoria and makes his rather radical theories known in press conferences. His political bosses are appalled. Prudence lies in distancing the party from his image or it may look like the party is trying to shield criminals within its fold. His name is unceremoniously dumped from the list of candidates. Naval is devastated by this reversal. Shruti suggests that they go on a vacation to ease the stress.

He decides that they should visit his hometown, the ancient city of Varanasi. Shruti visits relatives and the temples the city is famous for, while he wanders the streets, thinking about his past and planning for the future. One afternoon, in the old quarter, Naval feels drawn to a dimly-lit shop that sells antique books. A leather-bound book with gold-leaf trimmings catches his eye. It is an ancient copy of the *Ramayana*, probably one of the earliest English editions. The beautiful illustrations transport him to his childhood, when his grandfather had taken him to watch the Ramlila. The scenes and musical notes from those amateur renditions flood his mind. He feels compelled to buy the book. Shruti is vastly amused, for she's never known her husband, a man of logic, to be religious.

A few days later, they're back in Delhi where Naval is swamped with a backlog of cases. In his limited free time, he begins to read the *Ramayana*. Even though he has heard the story many times before, there is something mystical about the storytelling and the illustrations in this book. Soon he's reading it all the time at home. When Shruti kids him about his new hobby, he starts hiding the book between the pages of his files. He carries it to work and hides and reads it secretly. It's becoming an obsession.

That's when he learns about a lecturer who is touring Delhi. The man is a renowned archaeologist and historian who gives lectures on the Ramayana. Naval attends a lecture and is deeply enthralled by the historian who is a sagely figure – radiant and majestic in bearing and personality.

He stays back after the lecture and gets talking with the historian, Dr Devgupta. Naval is impressed by his profound understanding of the Ramayana and life in general. Devgupta can speak eloquently on any subject and Naval soon becomes a regular at his lectures. Soon they're discussing everything from philosophy and religion to society, relationships and even criminal law.

Devgupta encourages Naval to make a thesis of his work and enter it for the prestigious National Awards given for trailblazing work in various fields. That would be a fitting reply to those who've abandoned Naval. Devgupta even offers his time and resources to help Naval.

Naval, a brilliant man himself, realizes that the historian is the most charismatic person he has ever met. Starved of intellectual companionship, Naval soon starts treating him as his closest friend and confidant.

One day Naval reads a newspaper report that a team of archaeologists has found what it claims is the site of the ancient battle that is at the heart of the Ramayana. The site is in Sri Lanka, but the claims are a long way from being substantiated. That evening Devgupta appears disturbed. He asks Naval who, in his opinion, is Ramayana the story of? A sense of foreboding descends upon Naval. Like something major that was destined for him is about to take shape. When Naval hesitates to reply, Devgupta announces that, contrary to popular belief, the central character of the Ramayana is the much maligned demon king Ravana!

Naval is stunned and then wonders aloud whether the epic is based in reality at all and if those characters ever existed.

The historian smiles.'Oh! Ravana did exist. Just like it says in your book. And only his physical being died. His spirit is still alive.'

He says that even after thousands of years, Ravana's spirit can find no peace. Gross injustice has been done to him by generations through history.

He philosophizes that life is essentially the duality of all phenomena – evolution and involution, creation and destruction, good and evil. Good is only defined by the presence of evil. All morality on this earth owes its existence to evil. For isn't morality mostly defined by what not to do?

He says that even Ravana's visual image has been slashed and burnt and slandered at the level of the street: look at the billboards and graffiti-covered walls at hundreds of Ramlilas. But by burning him every year, people are only incarcerating the image of evil. And turning away guilt-free from the gut-wrenching task of dealing with the evil that resides within each one of them.

'All messengers of divinity are opposed by hostile forces. Men who can be misguided are found in every religion, every culture. Take the example of Jesus and Judas. Is Judas not important in making Jesus a martyr? And how unfairly history treats these men ... these sacrificial lambs. Ravana actualized Rama. His worship today is largely because of him, his sacrifice. But look how history has treated Ravana!' he says.

Centuries of pain appear to pour out on behalf of an entity that time has forsaken. For the first time, Naval's core beliefs are being challenged radically, and he is beginning to see the validity of his friend's argument.

Devgupta then says that he's been waiting for a genius like Naval to come along. Only Naval has the capability to set Ravana free and the vision to understand his thoughts. The time has come for evil to get justice. And if Naval believes in justice for all, now is the time to back his theories. He says that the newspaper report about the site of the battle being in Lanka is true. He wants Naval to go to the spot where Ravana's fossilized remains lie and recover his amulet. The amulet is an elixir of life. The amulet must be worn by Naval's wife!

He knows that Naval and Shruti have been trying to have children. A son will be born. Naval will be his earthly father. They will bring him up together. The child will have the inputs of two brilliant men. He will become a genius.

He wants the son to become a great lawyer, a master who will rescue sinners from further incarceration. No one should burn at the stake anymore. Only that will give him peace of mind.

A number of realizations sweep through Naval. Devgupta has always been a mystical figure without any family ties, swamped by his books and prone to dropping out of sight for days on end. Also, snatches of the animated outburst from Devgupta are in first person, spoken as if by Ravana himself.

Naval realizes that he was in the presence of some super phenomenon and that though the idea is outrageous, he doesn't flinch from it. At the time it seems like all genius. Outrageous, yes. But brilliant.

He travels to Sri Lanka and visits the site. He follows Devgupta's instructions and locates the fossil. He covertly extracts the special amulet.

With the pretext that something has been given to him to guard her precious pregnancy, he gives it to Shruti to wear. Shruti duly reports her pregnancy after a few weeks. Naval is ecstatic and when a son is born, Devgupta has tears of joy in his eyes. They name the boy Varana – an anagram of Ravana.

Even as a child, the boy has extraordinary charisma. He is clearly unique. His educational and other pursuits are carefully planned by Naval and the boy's other father. In time, Shruti starts feeling a little uncomfortable about the bonding between Naval and their son, especially since she is often ignored by them. Naval also deliberately keeps the boy away from temples and all religious scriptures.

Meanwhile, his thesis completed with Devgupta's help, is rejected as being too favourable to criminals. Naval feels dejected. His friend consoles him that he was passed over only because of the 'politics of the times'. He says of the jury: 'They're small men, Naval. They will never understand your vision.'

He quotes from the scriptures: 'The ruin of a society is not because of the absence of a sage, but because of a lack in making full use of one. Give your energies to where full use will be made of them. Immerse yourself in this cause.'

In time, the son enrolls in one of the leading law colleges

of the country. There is great emphasis at home on the importance of developing a sharp mind and becoming a winner. Naval helps him in attaining top grades.

He then delicately makes his son aware of his true identity. Varana is filled with pride at discovering that he's 'someone special'. Naval tells him all about the amulet that the boy has been wearing since he was born.

The son sets up a firm. In keeping with his fathers' vision, the firm takes up cases of corporate bosses and political figures in trouble.

As a lawyer, he is glib, articulate and cool, and is instantly successful. He employs like-minded people and trains them hard. They also become experts at handling mafia and crime syndicate cases. Soon, the firm has a branch in every city. It also acts as a power brokerage between warring mafia groups and political parties. Naval basks in his son's success and so does Devgupta. It is some time before Naval realizes that the frequency of his friend's visits has decreased, until one day he loses touch entirely with Devgupta.

The only person not kicked about all this is Shruti. She doesn't like the fact that her son works as a protector of criminals. But Naval brushes aside her fears.

One day, when Shruti just can't take it anymore, Naval decides to tell her the truth. Shruti is horrified. She breaks down and threatens to reveal their secret to the world. When Varana learns of this, he is furious. His work has just begun. His identity cannot be compromised.

He tells Naval that Shruti must be eliminated. Naval is stunned that his son would suggest this about his own mother. That's when Varana reminds him that he is not his real father. And his mission is more important than either of them. He threatens that if Shruti is not kept quiet, he will get rid of her and storms out of the house.

That's when Naval realizes what a colossal mistake he has made. He yearns for Devgupta to confer with, but he has stopped appearing. Naval goes into depression and falls ill. For many days Shruti nurses him. She reads to him from the old copy of the *Ramayana*. Shruti's pure and innocent interpretations of the same text open Naval's eyes.

'Can't you see what they've done, my love. They've taken the best amongst us and turned him to the dark side. They know that if they can convince you, they can convert anybody.'

He sees now that he has gone horribly wrong.

He desperately wants to make amends. Here again, Shruti guides him.

All his life, Naval has been a defense lawyer, thinking of it as a pursuit far superior to being a government prosecutor. He now has to launch a crusade against his son's work.

'Rescue our son,' Shruti begs him.

Naval, brilliant as ever, and burning with righteous indignation, starts working as a prosecutor. Time and again he thwarts his son's attempts to let a known criminal go free.

It builds up to a showdown as father and son confront each other. The case is of a high-profile syndicate boss and his son, who has been implicated in an arms-peddling case.The warehouse from where the arms were confiscated, is registered in the son's name. The boss has made it clear to Varana that neither he nor his son can ever go to prison because in Tihar jail are lodged members of an opposing gang with a sworn blood vendetta against them. Naval works very hard on the case, sensing that a victory could mean an effective end to the evil empire his son has created. He has many pitched legal battles in court against Varana. The fight is reminiscent of the great epic struggles, like the central conflict in the Ramayana itself. Naval is very close to getting a conviction. The boss panics and sends hit men to get him before the verdict is announced.

Naval, under police protection, survives but he is hospitalized. He is critically ill.

The mafia boss has acted out of haste without consulting Varana.

The media speculates that the judge could grant Naval a favourable verdict out of sympathy.

Varana senses that the case is slipping from his hands. His very survival is in jeopardy. He has to act quickly. It's time to make a few calls. And then to meet his father.

The sight of his father strapped to life support in the ICU is a disheartening one. Shruti then reminds him of a lifetime of caring and affection by Naval. He takes his mother's advice and turns away from Ravana. For the first time in his life, he enters a temple. The words of an ongoing discourse ring in his ears: 'The lord says, absolve all sinners. I promise you this, true repentance will never be rejected.'

For the first time, he takes off the amulet he has been wearing since birth.

He bows in repentance.

Varana tells Shruti that he knows the truth now and knows what to do.

He sabotages his own case. He proves that when the deed for the warehouse was signed, the boss's son was a minor and therefore not legally responsible. But his legal guardian at the time, his father, the boss, was responsible and thereby guilty.

When the boss is being taken away, he abuses Varana, saying that he'll be out on bail in a couple of days and then he'll get him. Varana informs him that he has made arrangements with the powers-that-be to take him straight to Tihar. He doubts if they'll ever hear from the boss again!

He visits Naval in hospital and tells him about the case. His father is drugged and talks about how he wasted a large part of his life in pandering to his ego. In pursuit of power and awards, intellectual honour without spiritual motivation, without the right faith or inspiration. He even made an alliance with the devil. He understood now, why he never succeeded.

Varana sympathizes with his father. Naval smiles.

'I don't care about positions and rewards now. What you have done today is the biggest prize I could get, that a son can give to his father, a man can give to another: a chance to atone for the sins of his past.'

As Varana's limo pulls away, Naval lies back and closes his eyes. At last he can rest. He drifts into sleep.

In the car, Varana reaches up and closes the partition

between him and the driver. He reaches for his cellphone.

His hand moves to his buttoned-up collar as he dials.

Deep in the bowels of the Tihar jail, a cellphone rings.

'It is done.' The voice is scratchy and wavering with the weakening signal.

'The court would have given him only a few years, we gave him what he deserved.'

Suddenly the signal becomes strong and the voice clear.

'Come and see me. We can work together, you and I.'

Varana slides the phone into his jacket pocket. He unbuttons his collar and strokes the coin-sized metal.

The amulet glints in the light of the evening sun. He looks outside at the world rolling by and closes his eyes. He settles back into the soft leather with a smile.

EPILOGUE

Naval dreams of a conversation he once had with Devgupta.

'What do you think, Naval, is evil's greatest trick on mankind?'

'I think, maybe, to show the world that it doesn't exist.'

Devgupta's usually intense features split in a smile. 'No, my friend. Evil's greatest trick on mankind is to show that it once existed but has since reformed!'

Naval comes awake. He struggles to shake off the deep slumber his body wants to lapse into. He must combat the lethargy of age and ill health. His feeble body trembles as if it is a battleground between good and evil. The monitors that Naval is strapped to start going wild, his pulse and BP rise, triggering an alarm. Shruti rushes to his bedside. She sees that he's awake. His first words to her are to bring him his briefcase.

'What's the urgency? Rest some more. Your battle is over, Naval.'

Naval pauses and shakes his head. 'I should have realized this when I decided to take on evil. There's going to be no rest for me. Evil will resurface in different forms, again and endlessly. It can never be destroyed because it is an inherent part of us. The battle against evil cannot be one decisive fight. Otherwise our gods and messiahs would have wiped it out long back. It has to be endless duels, day after day, for as long as we live and this world exists.'

Naval remembers Devgupta and their philosophical conversations. Devgupta often used to ask Naval how he thought evil could become powerful enough to rule the world.

Naval turns to his wife. Today, finally, the answer is clear.

'For evil to triumph, only one condition is necessary. That good should do ... nothing.'

He shuffles down the corridor, lawyer's robe over his shoulder and briefcase in hand. He turns around, smiles and waves to his wife, like any man off to do a day's work.

The Last Gurkha

Yubi loved stories. Especially the way Bauji told them. People from the hills were gifted storytellers – he had heard many stories in the past nine years – but there was no one who could spin a yarn like his grandfather did.

Bauji's stories were lively and bubbling, like a mountain spring full of twists and turns, and would mesmerize Yubi, leaving him craving for more.

Yubi's favourite time of day was the afternoon, when he would run back from school as fast as his spindly legs could carry him, and spend hours listening to the old man as he conjured up worlds of warriors, ghosts and fairies, princes and dragons. The afternoon sun bathed the brick house as it traversed their side of the hill and Bauji's voice, gravelly from years of smoking bidis, would cast its hypnotic spell. Yubi would slowly feel his eyelids droop and his last thought before he dozed off would be, Good, I'll be able to dream.

It was easy to dream after listening to Bauji.

Yubraj, or Yubi as everyone called him, was small for his age and when the sun became weak and winter came to the valley, he would often fall ill.

He didn't mind missing school because Bauji would wrap him in additional blankets and make sweet ginger tea and halwa for him. But the best part of falling ill was that stories would flow as a compensation. Unlike other grown-ups, Bauji was never in a hurry to finish a story or impatient about answering questions.

On those clear winter days, even though it was a struggle for him to breathe, he loved to run to the window and see the mist lift to reveal the mighty Kanchenjunga.

'Ah! See how it stands, steadfast like a soldier,' the old man would say and Yubi would immediately demand a story from Bauji's days as a soldier. Bauji's stories were about what he called The Great War in which they fought the fearsome Japanese in a place called Burma. This confused Yubi, for the Japanese tourists who trekked past their village to see the Junga were small and cute, bird-like creatures constantly bowing and bobbing about with their cameras.

Unlike other hill children who were tough and vigorous, Yubi was pale and knobby.

Bauji would often scold him.

'Stand tall, boy. Don't worry if you're short. Here, try standing at attention ... Chin up, back straight, like steel has passed through you from head to toe. Be like a soldier. It means, whatever the gods may throw at you, you are ready, and nothing will get through on your watch. Feel its power, beta.'

But try as he might, Yubi could never feel the spirit or purpose of any form of toughness. It was ironic, since most of the stories he liked or made up were about battles and warriors.

Yubi was a dreamer. He liked nothing better than to settle down with a piece of churpi and gaze at the hills till they became misty in the dusk. He would work on the cube of hard cheese, biting, sucking and gnawing for hours till it became paste. This time of lazy, unhurried reverie was when he would daydream his stories. Then with great enthusiasm he would narrate them to Bauji, who would look at him with pride.

'Maybe the prince should not be tall or strong, that's a little common in princes, isn't it? Maybe he should have a weakness so that we can all relate to him.'

On Mahashivratri, at the end of the day's celebrations, the entire village would gather around Bauji to hear his stories. With great pride Bauji would prod Yubi to narrate the introduction to the great Shiv–Parvati tale. That's when Yubi felt happiest.

The children in school would often give Yubi a hard time, jibing him about his small size and ill health.

They would call him 'Tingu' or 'Koff Koff' and mimic his constant cough.

On particularly bad days, after being bullied and chided by the other children, Yubi would loath to return to school.

'Come with me, Bauji. I feel scared to go to school alone.'

Bauji would respond instantly. He would pick up his mulberry walking stick and wear his old Gurkha felt hat. But he would never go into the school compound with Yubi.

'It's best I wait here, Yubi, near the old oak at the edge of the school. Your friends will only tease you more if they see me with you.'

Every now and then Yubi would peep from the classroom window and see the silhouette of Bauji's felt hat behind the tree and his fears vanished, just knowing Bauji was around.

But along came the Physical Education teacher Mr Temple and with him, a brand new threat – boxing.

Mr Temple had taken to teaching in schools aided by missionaries after he retired from the British army. This was his first teaching job, a village school in Darjeeling, and he pursued it with great military zeal.

When Temple first saw the gawky boy and the raw fear in his eyes, he yelled:

'Fall out, you! You're useless! Why do your knees knock like that eh, boy? Take those gloves off!'

He would say these things and the boys would poke fun at Yubi mercilessly for days.

Most of the times, when the other boys paired up for bouts, Temple left him out. Yubi didn't know what he hated more, the physical agony of boxing or the anguish of being left out.

The school was getting ready to celebrate its sports day. Everyone was excited about what Mr Temple had planned. But Yubi hated all sports – nothing highlighted his deficiencies more. He hated the way this new game of boxing was churning out its own cult of heroes and followers. Yubi wanted to be neither. He dreaded his time in the ring. Bruises and bloody lips were common and Yubi was petrified of blood, especially his own. His bouts were mostly spent furiously back-peddling from the fists of his opponent.

He looked upon the sports day with increasing alarm. Secretly, he had decided to be ill on that day. He was sure no one would miss him.

Temple, in a last-minute inspiration, decided to invite a team from a school in a neighbouring village to compete against theirs. This village was their traditional rival. When tourists had started flocking to the valley to take in the panorama of the Kunchenjunga, their neighbour had hogged most of the trade, only because the Member of the Legislative Assembly of this region was from there. He'd used his influence and got the Government Tourist Centre and resthouse constructed in his village.

So, for many years their neighbours had got rich off the tourist dollars and lorded their prosperity over Yubi's village. They had teasingly started calling Yubi's village a basti. That hurt, not just because the term alluded to squalor, but because it implied a rustic and backward mindset.

If the school boxing team could win the match, it would knock the conceit out of their neighbours forever.

When Temple compared the list of participants from both schools, he found one name on the other school's list that did not have an opponent's name marked against it. Only one boy could match that boy's size and weight. It was Yubi.

Temple didn't mind. He was sure his champs would win the contest for him long before Yubi's turn came. That bout would just be some light entertainment for all at the end.

Yubi prayed earnestly for his asthma to invade his lungs, but for once his chest heaved rhythmically minus any sawing or whistling noises.

Bauji understood Yubi's torment. 'You always have a choice, my son. You can duck out of this boxing match, but then you'll spend your entire life ducking. To be brave isn't tough. You have to be strong here,' Bauji said, tapping Yubi's head.

'Here, look at me. I'm not that strong or tall, and when I was young, I used to fall ill all the time, like you. But I learnt something in the army. You can never be brave for yourself. You have to find a bigger purpose than yourself. Find that, and you will always be brave.'

Yubi detected the beginning of a story here.

'Were you a brave soldier, Bauji?'

'Ah, of course I was, my child. You can ask Irrawaddy. She knows how I made her blush that day.' The old man chortled as he took a deep drag on his bidi.

Yubi knew that when the old man got that misty look in his eyes and got busy with his hookah, he would go to a far off place from where nothing came except stories.

One day before the sports day, Bauji took out the trunk he kept under his bed. The trunk was a treasure trove. The sum of Bauji's life. Like his stories, the trunk was a mysterious place.

It was crammed full of old books and letters, badges and colourful military ribbons, even a ceremonial khukhri in a scabbard. Once, when rummaging through it, Yubi had dug out a small box covered with a silk cloth. Inside was a bronze object shaped like a cross he'd seen in a church. He had looked in awe at the exquisite craftsmanship.

'What is it, Bauji? Is it a prayer gong of the Christians?'

Bauji had smiled but not answered his question.

That day, Bauji held up the piece for him and said, 'I know you love it, Yubi. You can have it if you win tomorrow.'

Yubi knew the chances of that happening were minimal.

On the morning of the sports day, Yubi got up early, having hardly slept at all. His mother had prepared halwa–poori, his favourite breakfast. He could scarcely touch it. His stomach felt like it was full of sour curd.

He went to see his grandfather. Normally, Bauji would leave for his morning walk the same time Yubi left for school. Today, Bauji's walking stick was leaning against the wall.

'Bauji's not well, Yubi,' his mother told him.

Yubi peered inside the room.

He went up to the figure swathed in blankets. The wrinkles on his grandfather's face seemed to have increased.

Suddenly, Bauji opened his eyes. He raised himself on an elbow.

'Ready, Yubi? Good. Remember the key to bravery.'

Yubi nodded.

'A purpose bigger than yourself.' Bauji smiled.

'And also that gong from your trunk,' Yubi added.

Bauji laughed and lay back.

'Go ... You will have no fear.'

Yubi hesitated.

'What is it?'

'Can you come today, Bauji?'

Bauji replied straight away.

'Of course I'll come, my child, it's your big day. I'll be at my usual place behind the tree.' Bauji winked.

Yubi felt on top of the world now that Bauji was going to be there.

There was a festive air about the school that day. Colourful paper buntings festooned the arena. The small courtyard was full of people.

With the clang of a hammer on a footlong track of rail that served as the bell, the competition began.

Temple and the master from the other school were rooted in their respective corners, urging, cajoling and often threatening their wards to better effort.

But soon it became clear that the teams were evenly matched. In a couple of hours, they had run down their ranks, the crowd had cheered themselves hoarse, the two masters had almost come to blows themselves, and there was still no clear winner.

At last there were just two participants left – Yubi and his opponent. Now there was no way out.

Yubi had often heard Bauji say as he counselled the village folk on some issue, that a man may get away from anything but his fate.

When Yubi stepped into the ring, his entire school fell silent. They knew they might as well hand the victory to the other school.

Temple was imparting all kinds of last-minute tactics, but Yubi was so nervous that he couldn't hear a thing. He kept looking towards the far end of the ground, at the old oak.

Was Bauji there?

And there, behind the stooping, aged oak, he saw the familiar silhouette that had instantly calmed him dozens of times before. Bauji's Gurkha felt hat.

Yubi felt better. He looked at his opponent. The boy looked like a pit bull raring to go.

When the bell rang, the boy came at Yubi at a fast pelt. Yubi imagined that he was snarling.

Yubi started back-peddling, desperate to avoid the other boy's pumping fists, but soon the boy had cornered him. The first punch that bruised him was a left hook, followed by a flashing right. The one that drew blood was an upper cut.

Yubi had never known such pain. He opened his mouth but no scream came. He saw the boy jumping up and down, arms in the air, doing a victory dance already as his schoolmates cheered.

Suddenly he came at Yubi again and Yubi never even saw the roundhouse punch as his knees caved in. He felt he was in a tunnel. Why was he lying down?

He felt the rough canvas mat rubbing against his face. He blinked to clear his vision.

He saw the faces of his friends. They looked tired, defeated, utterly disappointed. As if they all knew that he was worthless.

He imagined some of them moving away.

He hadn't realized how important this match was to them, to the whole village.

One of the faces called out, 'Come on, Yubi!'

It caught on like a chorus.

'Come on, Yubi!'

'Shabash, Yubi!'

They were counting on him. He was their last hope.

A purpose bigger than yourself, my boy.

Through the film of tears streaming from his eyes and nose, he saw the old man's hat behind the tree again. Thank God, Bauji was there. He was watching. I must get up.

There was a sigh of disappointment from the other team when Yubi rose.

His legs were trembling, he couldn't feel his lips, and he was pretty sure that a tooth had come loose.

He imagined he saw Bauji again. The time when the old man had posed for him with the khukhri from his trunk. He saw his grandfather command his frail and arthritic body to stand erect. He saw him shrug off old age and infirmity. He saw him assume the strike position of a Gurkha warrior, khukhri in hand. When his grandfather yelled the dreadful battle cry, 'Ayo gurkhali!' Yubi had shivered.

'See how the Kanchenjunga stands, my boy, like steel from head to toe.'

He could see the mighty mountain in the backdrop.

On your watch, nothing will get through ... nothing.

A purpose bigger than yourself.

Yubi's puffy lips formed the words 'Ayo gurkhali ... ayo gurkhali ... Steadfast, the gurkhas ...'

He took up a defensive stance. The other boy looked puzzled. He hesitated, straining to hear the words Yubi was whispering. Then he came at Yubi. Fists pumping, he unleashed a barrage of blows.

Left, right, left, right, upper cut.

Those present that day saw something that they would talk about even years later.

Yubi just stood still and took each blow.

Every single person in the crowd flinched with the crashing sounds.

Mr Temple considered ending the bout, but something in Yubi's demeanour stopped him.

Yubi's face was bruised the colour of raw meat, his lips bled, yet he stood.

The other boy was bewildered.

Yubi's schoolmates started cheering ... They saw hope.

When the boy came at Yubi again, he was looking deflated. Another couple of blows and his arms hung to his sides in exhaustion. He was panting. Yubi stood still.

The boy looked at Yubi's eyes, they seemed to be looking beyond him. The boy tipped his head to follow his gaze. Yubi seemed to be staring at the Kanchenjunga.

The boy, drenched in sweat and completely spent, just stood there, now unable to move.

With a huge effort, Yubi moved his gloved fist back.

'Ayo gurkhali!'

From where, he didn't know, he summoned the energy for a blow. Just one blow ... That's all he needed.

The punch caught the boy in his jaw, his eyes rolled, he hit the mat.

Led by Temple, Yubi's schoolmates carried him on their shoulders all the way back to his house that day. He was the hero who had saved the honour of the village.

The pain was unbearable, but Yubi had never been happier.

As the procession neared Yubi's house, they saw a throng of people gathered there. They were standing in silence with their heads hung.

His mother ran up to him.

'Yubi! Oh, Yubi!' She hugged him and started crying.

'Yubi … Bauji has left us,' she finally said.

Yubi turned and stared at the body covered by a white sheet on a bier, ready for cremation.

Yubi started to tremble.

'He wanted you to have this, Yubi.' She handed him the silk-covered box.

Temple put a hand on his shoulder.

Yubi opened the box containing the gong.

'My god!' Temple whispered, staring at the cross in awe.

He took the box from Yubi's hand.

'Whose is this?'

'My grandfather's,' Yubi whispered.

'Do you know what this is, Yubi? It's the greatest medal ever given to a warrior. It means the recipient is a great hero.' Taking the simple bronze medal out of the box, he said, 'This is a Victoria cross!' He held it like a religious object.

He took out a folded piece of paper stuck to the bottom of the box. It contained a citation. None in the village could read English fluently except Mr Temple.

'Awarded to Sepoy Lachmann Bir Rai of the Gurkha Regiment for conspicuous gallantry and bravery above and beyond the call of duty in face of the enemy.

'On 21 June 1942, on the banks of the Irrawaddy river in Burma, sepoy Lachmann single-handedly held off an entire troop of Japanese after his whole company had been killed.

'Through the night the sepoy, in spite of suffering from numerous wounds, did not surrender his post.

'In an ingenious tactic, the sepoy propped up the rifles of his fallen comrades with their hats atop to give the enemy the impression that they were facing far more men.'

Yubi was crying. He imagined a young gurkha all alone, surrounded by the enemy, his blood mingling freely with the waters of the river, khukhri in hand, the chant of 'Ayo gurkhali!' on his lips.

As they picked up Bauji's body, a wail arose from the village folk.

It looked like the old warrior's body had come to attention. His face was at peace, as if a great mission had been accomplished.

Yubi's mother put her hand on Yubi's head.

'When did this happen?' he asked.

'Soon after you went to school, he wanted to go out. We tried to stop him, but he wouldn't listen, then he was back in a few minutes and soon after that he was gone.'

'But how can this be? I saw Bauji … He came to see my match.'

'No, he didn't.'

'He did, he did. I saw him. I saw him …'

Yubi suddenly fell silent.

He ran as fast as he could to the oak tree near his school.

Planted in the mud, swaying in the breeze, was Bauji's walking stick and on top of it, the familiar gurkha felt hat.

Through his tears Yubi started smiling.

He saw Bauji's bier pass through the village and people followed.

Yubi wiped away his tears and came to attention like Bauji had taught him.

The last gurkha was passing.

God's Hand

His day began early, the time the Hindus call uday, the time that the sahib rose and had to be served tea.

Handling coal and stoves was not worthy of a man born into a high caste. But the firangi sahib had no idea about this and Dinanath, even after so many years, had never been able to explain the strict workings of the caste system to him. In fact, he had never been able to explain Shiva and Vishnu and the other thousand gods that virtually ran a Hindu's life.

The sahib, David Pringle, was a huge man. His fleshy face, red and blotchy from the tropical sun and insect bites, looked down on the natives from a height of over six feet, always locked in a scowl. But despite his looks, the sahib was a decent man who looked after his servants. The sahib treated all of them like his children. Which was good if you were a child, but infuriating if you had children of your own, like Dinanath had. Since his birth, Dinanath's faith had been his life, his identity. They were beyond examination or negotiation.

But the sahib often chided Dinanath about his beliefs and his religion, terming them superstitions and steeped in rituals. The sahib wanted an explanation for everything. How does one explain that Shiva's tandav could destroy the whole world, to someone who believed that there was just one god, who resided in a couple of pieces of wood nailed together?

He poured just a few drops of milk into the tea. Why did the sahib drink this dark concoction? Why no sugar and no milk? These firangis had strange tastes. And what did they have against milk anyway? It was cow's milk ... Good for your body and mind. Didn't the Hindu scriptures say so? But he had heard dark tales that the firangis ate cows in their land. Rama, Rama!

No, it couldn't be. Only demons ate cows. For as soon as you ate a cow, you would transform into a demon. Everyone knew that.

How poor and backward this village was, only one well and the solitary temple with just one idol. No wonder these villagers lived in squalor. What the hell was he, a high-caste Brahmin, doing in this tribal village?

He asked himself this each time. As if the answer would change. Fact was that his sahib was a hunter and would go wherever a contract sent him. As the gun-bearer, he had to be at the sahib's side throughout the hunt. Dinanath would not have hung on for a minute but, hai ree kismet, the money was good and it was getting very difficult to make a living off birth and death ceremonies as Brahmins traditionally did. There were not enough people being born or dying, or maybe there were just too many Brahmins.

But this time, the prey was different. This time they were after Gajraj – a rogue elephant who had been decimating crops and human beings alike. Finally the harried villagers from the district had got together and hired his sahib. This was the first time they were hunting an elephant and David sahib was excited. But Dinanath could find nothing exciting about the prospect.

Firstly, tigers and panthers were the denizens of the forest, they were demons in disguise and though hunting them was terrifying work, it was good karma to bring them down. But elephants ... The elephant was Ganesha, the elephant god, the son of Lord Shiva himself. Dinanath had worshipped Shiva twice daily since the day he uttered his first words. Even contemplating killing this holy vehicle was a sin.

Secondly, Dinanath was petrified by the mere description of this elephant. They said he was so large that when he stood in front of you, he blocked the sun. His tusks were mammoth columns of ivory as big as the pillars of the Shiva temple at Benaras. He had also heard that Gajraj had a violent hatred of humans ever since he had been shot at and wounded by a native hunter's musket.

The idea of confronting such a large and angry beast and that too, a favourite of the gods, was daunting indeed. The gods worked in mysterious ways. A human could just pray and make offerings everyday to keep them happy.

Suddenly, there was a sharp acrid smell in the air. Dinanath turned around. There he was! Just like that. His nut-brown face split in a grin and his small eyes came alive and twinkled. It was Nandi the tracker, a gnome-like figure, not much taller than a child. He was a creature of the forest itself. He had been sent in three days back to track Gajraj. Chuckling and drooling, he patted his small balloon-like belly, looking pointedly at the pot of bubbling rice khichdi.

'Always hungry,' Dinanath muttered. 'Shoo! I'll give you some when it's ready,' he yelled.

Shaitan, he thought, how many times I've told him not to come near the kitchen area.

Nandi was a tribal and therefore of an indeterminate caste. Too much contact with him could make a person unclean.

Dinanath observed that the canvas shoes that had been given to Nandi were tied around his neck. He had been using them to store things. From one of the shoes, he brought out a wad of tobacco. Tobacco was the only currency known to Nandi. His pay and rewards were just measures of tobacco.

Nandi was the sahib's favourite. In this form of work, a good tracker was priceless. And Nandi was the best. He had this unique gift of being able to track any animal, even if the spoor was a few days old.

'I've seen Gajraj,' he whispered. 'His tusks are so huge that they plough the earth!'

Dinanath didn't know when to take Nandi seriously and always suspected he was pulling his leg. Damn the half-caste!

He remembered that a one-eyed, dark-skinned trader from Bombay had visited the sahib a couple of months back.

'David sahib, the future is in ivory. Skins and fur are common now. Get me ivory. My clients are hungry for it. I'll get you five hundred rupees a gramme.'

He saw the betelnut-stained mouth utter those words and ensnare his sahib.

Hai Ram! The kala admi was sending them to ruination.

'So will you be able to find this Gajraj again?'

Nandi shook his head. In between blowing on the steaming khichdi, he said, 'It's a very thick forest. He could be here or a hundred miles away and we wouldn't know ... Why do you look so happy?'

'I hope that you never find that elephant and the sahib can never kill the symbol of Ganesha.' Dinanath touched his ears to ward off even the effect of the suggestion of his evil words.

'Oh, has your karma come knocking, Brahmin?' Nandi grinned.

'Shut up! What do you know about karma!'

'I don't, but I know that no elephant means no bonus.'

Nandi was right, and this time the sahib had promised them fifty rupees each.

It was a tough choice – karma verses fifty rupees. He felt weak. Money would trump karma as it usually did.

Nandi had devoured two bowls of khichdi and was rolling a second wad of tobacco when suddenly he started smiling.

'What are you feeling so good about, you tribal fool?'

'I know how we can get our fifty rupees and also keep your gods happy.'

'How?'

Without replying, Nandi took to his mat and turned in for the night.

'We have an early start tomorrow, O high born one. It's ten miles to the temple in the next village.'

It was midday when they reached their destination. This village was almost the size of a town. In the centre stood an imposing temple with a fifty-foot-high copula. Nandi led Dinanath to the back of the temple. A large shadow filled the yard.

'Look, Brahmin, it's Gajraj!'

A huge tusker stood there, unfettered and docile, smacking sugarcane stalks against its legs before devouring them whole. A string of bells hung from its neck.

'This is a temple elephant, not Gajraj. Are you making a fool of me?'

'Of course it's not Gajraj. We know that, but does the sahib?'

'Are you mad? Gajraj is a rouge elephant. This one is meek like a puppy.'

'You know what it takes to drive him to rage? Just this, mixed in his sugarcane.' Nandi was holding a green chilli, the short, thin variety known for its punch.

'But can we control him after that?'

'Of course. He was born in captivity. There's nothing wild about him. He'll stomp the ground, flare his ears and trumpet like crazy, but he won't harm anyone. He's available for twenty rupees a day ... Come, let's have a hookah with his mahout and work out our plan.'

It was a good deal. They'd spend twenty and make a hundred.

The next day, the sahib burst out of his tent, Nandi walking behind him. 'Come on! Get ready to go. The little bugger has found the elephant. Dina! Check the guns again.' The sahib never called him by his full name. It was either Dina or Nath. Only a child's name is shortened. He couldn't understand why the sahib always shortened his.

Half-crouched, Nandi led them into the dense forest. The sahib walked close behind him. To the sahib's right was Dinanath. The sahib had taught them to keep their 'hunting formation' regardless of the pace. The sahib carried the double-barrelled shotgun and Dinanath, the more powerful express rifle. In case the game got in too close, the sahib would switch guns.

Deep in the forest, Nandi waved them back and melted away into the undergrowth. After a few minutes he appeared again. He told them that the elephant was just a few yards ahead. Luckily, the wind direction favoured them.

Dinanath felt nervous, he wasn't sure the plan would work. The sahib knew the creatures of the forest. If he suspected something, Dinanath would surely lose his job. Why had he listened to Nandi?

He decided to pray to Shiva for their success.

'Om Namo Shiva, Om Namo Shiva,' he whispered.

'Check the load, Dina,' the sahib called out.

He opened the breech of the rifle.

He looked at the two brass cartridges in the breech. The jungle was dense and humid and his sweat, streaming freely now, was getting into his eyes. He noticed for the first time that the bullets were shaped like Shivlings. Shaken with this divine revelation, he reached for them.

Suddenly, wild trumpeting filled the air.

The earth shuddered and instantly the elephant was upon them.

For a moment no one reacted. Then Nandi, as per plan, scurried away into the bush. Even though he was prepared for it, Dinanath stood rooted to the spot, completely paralyzed. Outside the domestic setting, the temple elephant seemed bigger and more menacing. The sahib turned to him and grabbed the rifle from his hands. The high-powered rifle was their only hope, if at all. Dinanath stood shivering as the forest in front of them erupted and the elephant emerged, large as a mountain.

Dinanath looked up and saw a stream of liquid running down the side of the elephant's face. Hai Ram! It was in mast ... That time of the year when an elephant's hormones raged! Nice touch! It must have been the work of Nandi and the mahout to enhance the effect for the sahib.

The eyes were fiery orbs of blazing hatred. Probably reddened with kohl. Nandi had managed quite a theatrical production. It was his part now.

Dinanath restarted his chant.

'Om Namo Shiva!' He was shouting now, hands folded in prayer at the sight before him. The sahib aimed the gun and fired. The answering click was a dry sound. He pulled the bolt back and fired again.

Another click.

'Dinanath!' he yelled, whether in shock or in anger,

Dinanath would never know. It was the first time that the sahib had called him by his full name.

Dinanath fell to his knees. Whether the sahib's legs gave way or he blindly followed Dinanath's actions is not known, but suddenly he too was kneeling beside Dinanath. Dinanath's voice was clear as never before.

'Om Namo Shiva ... Om Namo Shiva ...'

The shadow of the trunk that could crush them with one blow flitted over their heads.

Incredibly he heard another voice join the lilt of the incantation – the sahib's.

He was uttering words in his own language, his hands moving feverishly making the cross sign of his god.

Their voices lifted, instinctively groping for harmony as if their merger was their only hope. The trembling tone built up to a din. It seemed to go on forever.

The massive shadow of the trunk came closer till he felt a brief touch. Dinanath looked up and saw it gently caress them as if to establish a connection. The twin pillars of ivory that could impale them in an instant nudged them. Then Gajraj moved his tusks back carefully. Dinanath saw that the elephant was deliberately and gently avoiding a termite hill.

Massive padded feet shuffled and gradually moved away.

He looked up. The elephant's eyes seemed to be glazed as if in a trance. The manic gleam was gone. The effect of the chilli had diminished and the chanting it had heard all its life had calmed it, just as Nandi had said.

As Gajraj started to turn away, Dinanath looked for the

giveaway mark on its forehead. The temple branding which the mahout had claimed he could erase with a pumice stone. He couldn't see it. Good then, nor could the sahib.

Dinanath's fist was still clenched, almost of its own will. He opened it. The two shiny cartridges rolled in the cup of his sweaty palm. The sahib was still in a zombie-like stupor and muttering to himself, maybe remembering some long-forgotten prayer.

He quietly slipped the bullets back into the breech. The idea was to let the sahib think the gun had misfired.

The next day, Nandi and Dinanath went to the village temple. Eagerly they held out two ten-rupee notes to the mahout.

He looked at the money quizzically, then folded his hands.

'Please forgive me for yesterday, brothers. You know it was the village headman's function. I couldn't say no to the mukhiyaji. The elephant was needed there. But fix any other day and I'll bring the elephant and leave him in that grove in the forest you showed me. I'll even do it for half price.'

They froze. Then Nandi's back suddenly gave way and he sat down on his haunches. Dinanath backed away slowly. He didn't realize it, but Nandi was chanting. 'Om Namo Shiva.'

It was an accepted practice in those days to release temple elephants into the wild once they became old. Unable to fend for themselves, a number of them turned rogue.

David Pringle went through a mystical transformation after this incident. He lobbied hard with the British government and got permission to fence in a large tract of the forest. Here he forbade hunting. The site was the humble beginning of the now famous Dhudwa National Park. Pringle never returned to England. India ensnared him forever. He found religion. Many years after India became free, people would flock to Kangra – a hamlet in the foothills of the Himalayas – to visit the hut of a large, red-faced Englishman swaddled in the robes of a swami. The locals called him 'firangi baba'.

One amongst his visitors would insist on calling the ascetic 'sahib', and smile happily at being addressed only as 'Dina', or sometimes 'Nath'.

And from afar one could hear the discourse, the good word, not restricted to any one faith, being spread in a loud booming voice. The sermon would always end with words from 'the book' and someone called Peter.

'Humble yourselves, ye all. Under God's hand.'

And even after all those years, Dinanath's fist would clench in automatic reflex around the two brass cartridges he always carried in his pocket like a good luck charm.

Bata Shoes

9 a.m.
6 September 1965

The land seemed to crouch low on the horizon to receive us as we came over the rise. We swayed and bucked over the furrowed fields. If a thirty-five tonne tank could be made to tiptoe, we were doing it. We wanted to be very quiet. In the tall stalks of the sugarcanes, the water tower of the abandoned village or even from the sky above, danger lurked everywhere.

The bridge ahead seemed unmanned. Was this a trap?

Grey water surged and foamed in the brick-lined canal. Across that water lay Pakistan.

'Charger One crossing canal,' I said on the radio to the five tanks behind mine.

All warrior customs are steeped in primitive vocabulary and ritual. Ancient warriors used to paint themselves as animals in a bid to imbibe their strength and prowess. We don't do that anymore, but ... we paint symbols on our machines and hope for the same effect. The insignia painted on the sides of our tanks was of a charging horse, the symbol of our regiment, and so we were chargers one through six. We could have easily called ourselves tank one, two, three etc., but what the hell! 'Charger' sounded so much better.

To be Charger One was to have mixed feelings. I was tired of being three or four all the time. It felt good to be going up the pecking order.

The downside was this: in a battle, there is a one in four chance of being hit. But to be the leading tank on an advance, forget it, nobody could give you the odds of survival on that. The Americans apparently took turns at being lead. If a tank survived the day, it would rotate to the end of the column and another took its place. No such thing here. The Indian Army still insists on its commanders leading. It's why we lose a lot of officers and that 'number one' spot falls vacant so often. I'm a big fan of the American system.

We came off the bridge and our tracks spat out chunks of tar. The road seemed to have seen it all before. Dozens of armies had traversed the G.T. Road for hundreds of years. It was the artery that pumped lifeblood into the heart of Pakistan. It may not be the capital, but the city that lay ahead was the soul of this land, the essence of its people. We could almost feel the throbbing of that great heart.

Forty kilometres ahead stood Lahore.

Lahore, from where, eighteen years ago, my family had been thrown out. I remembered it all vividly. The home of my ancestors packed into two loosely tied bundles. I kept wondering why we were taking clothes for the dhobi. Pitaji telling us three brothers to be brave and Maaji sobbing quietly on the railway platform. The crowds and the mad rush for the trains. I was seven, but I recollect a lot from that train ride to Amritsar. The crush, the grime and the hunger, the wails and cries, and most of all, the look in everybody's eyes, like the eyes of a crazed dog cornered by men. I didn't understand what was going on, but I heard the word on everybody's lips: partition.

The word brought out a look on Pitaji's face I'd never seen before. Years later, I came to know it as loss. The loss of livelihood and dignity, but mostly of hope. My father had a traditional Punjabi's sense of izzat. In Lahore, Pitaji was somebody. He had a good job and the respect of his peers. In India, he was just another refugee. He never really recovered from the Partition.

The foliage on the sides of the road suddenly came alive with soldiers. Thankfully they were our own troops waiting for us so that they could advance further with our support. They cheered when they saw us. Hardy lads of yeoman stock from Haryana and Rajasthan, the Jats looked upbeat, even though they'd been at it since last night and had lost a lot of guys when they'd breached the border at Atari. Take away the helmets, guns and kit, and they looked like kids on a picnic.

One of their officers waved and grinned. He was looking at the regimental sign on the side of my tank.

'Scindia horse! Ha! Welcome to the party, boys!'

Ha! he wasn't going to outdo me in the chest thumping. I hate bravado but I know how to hunt with the hounds, at least figuratively.

'Party starts now, friend!' I said.

We started down the road. The six tanks led the way and the infantry fanned out around us. We progressed slowly, moving our guns continuously to keep all areas covered. Ahead lay open ground. A soldier always fears open ground.

I've always believed that it's better for a commander to be prudent. The glory hunters might appear glamorous but they give their men ulcers and scarcely get anything done.

Earlier, our tanks had been picked up by the Paki anti-tank guns as we crossed open ground and then slowed down to cross the triple railway lines coming out of the junction at Safila. The hedges and trees near the railway station, had seemed to spit shells at us.

It was the first time most of us had seen combat. We learnt that tanks were far from being the invulnerable beasts we imagined them to be. They were actually egg-like, with deceptively strong outer shells and a mushy inner core. If hit, our remains would have to be scrapped off. Whatever glory or virtue I'd imagined about battle was history. I'd lost friends there.

A tank being hit in battle was a violent intrusion in the lives of men who lived cheek by jowl for long periods of time. Tank crews shared everything: food, clothes, body odour, stories, good news and bad. When tanks burnt, so did these carefully nurtured relationships.

It was dangerous to stop, but I had to check our position on the map. This journey was unplanned, we didn't even know how accurate our maps were. Nobody expected us to be so deep in Pakistan, heading for Lahore – not our side and certainly not the Pakis.

When the Pakistani Army had worked out their

formations in this war, they'd come up with an audacious plan. A massive force of the dreaded American-made Patton tanks had been sent to launch an attack on Punjab. They wanted to cross the Beas river before we could react. If they did that, the route to Delhi, a one-day drive, would be virtually clear. The only place we could stop them then was, strangely enough at Panipat. Remember Panipat? Historically, each battle at Panipat has changed India's fate.

However, in all their manoeuvres, a tiny crack had appeared. An area, just a few miles wide, where their forces did not overlap. A small troop of our infantry and tanks took advantage of this and slipped through to the road to Lahore.

I wasn't kicked about this. I thought it was unnecessary bravado. All we had to do was go on the defensive, dig in, slug it out for a few days and wait for the superpowers to twist the ears of errant politicians, ours and theirs. All this dashing about would achieve nothing and get people killed.

I unfolded the next square of my folded map. Each square of the map represented sixteen kilometres on the ground. The map showed G.T. Road curving to the right and a couple of kilometres ahead was the sign of a shed marked 'Factory'.

I called brigade headquarters to ask if they wanted me to keep going.

'Any opposition?' the Brigadier asked.

'Not yet.'

'Then carry on, regardless!'

Regardless? It was easy to be regardless when you

were sipping steaming hot chai in the comfort of a tent far away from action.

The road ahead was devoid of trees, shrubs or any other cover. Our biggest threat was perhaps from the air. It was only a matter of time before a patrolling Paki Sabrejet caught us. We knew it was not easy for a fighter jet to hit a tank with a rocket. But the Sabres carried fifty kilogramme rockets. Sixteen of them. A direct hit on a tank would be gruesome. All of us knew the chances of surviving that were very small.

It was stupidity to continue on the open road. All my instincts rebelled against it. Honestly, I don't even pretend to have the instincts of a devil-may-care superhero. I sometimes wonder where the dash and disdain for danger comes from in men. I suspect that a man's greatest fear is showing it, especially in front of his comrades. I think a lot of heroism is actually the fear of shame. Men are ready to kill and die so as not to die of embarrassment. The same quality that Pitaji had always wanted to protect: his izzat.

Well I don't make for a very heroic figure. I'm short and slight and I wear spectacles. I've never been a sportsman and am as unlikely a candidate for the army as any. I watched Humphrey Bogart's *Sahara* at Rivoli Cinema in Delhi as a kid and had fantasized about tanks ever since. Pitaji was convinced I'd fail dismally in the army. He didn't understand that the army was his youngest son's way of gaining some respect, some izzat, from two older, bigger and sportier brothers.

From here on, we'd have to move with our top hatch closed. Claustrophobia is pronounced in a tank when the hatch is closed. Our Sherman tanks were not designed for comfort. The commander, gunner, driver and loader occupied an iron cave five feet across. From here I could see the world only through my periscope. One had to sense rather than see what was happening. The acrid engine fumes and heat made you suffer from persistent thirst. This was our world. We hated it. We loved it.

This thirty-five tonne hunk of metal was our protection. There was a certain homeliness about it. Letters were tucked behind the radio set, tins of precious condensed milk were stored on the sides, cigarette packets were stacked next to the gun breech, the only place that was always dry. But the crew's most prized possession was a calendar cutout of Lord Shiva pasted behind the driver's seat. They lit incense sticks everyday and made absurd promises to god, to be fulfilled if they managed to survive. I'm not a believer and became even more sceptical when I heard Dhani Ram, the gunner, chant his prayers. He was a Brahmin. After the preliminary invocations to the gods, his aarti would come quickly down to business.

'Protect us, Mahadev, from the rockets of the Sabre, the anti-tank shells, the 90 mm gun of the Patton tank.'

The rest of the crew would join in with cries of 'Har Har Mahadev!' while he blew incense smoke all over the tank to seal the pact with Shiva.

In spite of doing two aartis that day, we were discovered. The soldiers ahead were pointing upwards. I asked the driver to stop. We could hear a soft rumble across the sky and then I saw it glint like a speck of silver. A Sabrejet fighter of the Pakistani air force.

'What the hell should we do?' the other tank commanders were asking.

What the hell could we do? There was no place to hide. We were screwed!

The jet came at us incredibly fast, leaving the sound of its engines far behind.

'Split!' I yelled over the radio. It was a preplanned move. In case we were attacked from the air, all six tanks would scoot off in different directions, presenting a confusing target.

It was a pretty rudimentary ruse, but it worked. The Sabre seemed to go for the supply vehicles behind us. Suddenly, there was a twinkling of lemon-yellow on the Sabre's nose and the sky was filled with a hundred lashing whips. Then it lowered its nose and fired a salvo of rockets. Shrieking, they came, leaving trails of smoke behind. The tanks managed to get clear of the trucks before the rockets hit.

Even in my faraway tank the explosions sounded like a giant hammer had bludgeoned the world. Most of the trucks went up with a deafening crump as our stock of food, ammunition and fuel caught fire.

The jet came back for a second pass. This time the whooshing of the rockets and the explosions sounded close. The Saber must have been just twenty–thirty metres high. The tank seemed to rock in its wake. Oh, god! Did he have us in sight? When the sound abated, we could hear each other gasping for air. I looked at the crew. Everyone was motionless, silent, hunched over, mouth open, so that our eardrums wouldn't burst. All of us scared shitless.

As if in slow motion, frame by frame, the world took on its old logic; absolute silence, then wind, then sunlight, then voices. I opened the hatch and peeked outside. The jet was gone.

Thick smoke was billowing from the column of our supply trucks. In place of the first four trucks were twisted and charred metal skeletons. I wasn't worried about food and water, we could live off the land. The bastard had got our fuel. Tanks are guzzlers and without fuel we were done for. My first thought should have been for the safety of the truckers. It wasn't. It was this, that without enough diesel, could we get back to our side and safety? Shouldn't we be turning back right away?

I began to question the idea of war again, intensely and abusively, only for the hundredth time. Not this war, just all bloody wars.

Awkwardly, the men were reassembling themselves, first privately, then in groups ... becoming soldiers again.

A jeep sent for reconnaissance ahead had returned and was reporting to their boss, a colonel of the infantry. This guy was a real John Wayne-type figure. He sat on the bonnet of his jeep and smoked filterless cigarettes throughout the air attack. The nonchalance was disturbing to me, but he was a big hero to his men.

The recon team came up to me and opened out their field map.

'There's a factory ahead. About five kilometres down

the road. Appears to have been abandoned in a hurry. Beyond that, the road to Lahore seems clear!'

Could also be a bloody trap, I thought.

'Any anti-tank ditches or signs of freshly dug up earth in the area?' I asked.

'Do you mean, have they laid mines? Difficult to tell for sure.'

I looked at the colonel. I had to do it. I had to lie with a straight face. This nonsense had gone on long enough. In the end, they'd be thankful for my lie.

'Sir, the tanks are pretty low on fuel, I think this is the time to turn back. We could be heading into a trap. If we go further, we may not have fuel to return. Besides, we've already advanced further than anyone expected us to.'

The colonel hesitated. But finally my logic tipped the scales for him.

'Okay, let's get ready to move out.'

I deflated with relief.

I turned to go and asked them over my shoulder, 'What factory was it?'

To this day, I don't know why I asked the question. I didn't really want an answer. It was like a conversation filler, something to distract the others from my panic, nothing more. The answer changed my world.

'It's a shoe factory. The Bata shoe factory,' the colonel said and started moving towards the jeep.

I stood rooted to the ground, unable to move, unable to breathe.

Bata shoe factory.

Words I'd heard my entire life. Words that were part of our family like an heirloom. Pitaji could not string together more than a few sentences without the mention of Bata shoes or the Bata shoe factory in Lahore. He'd gone to work there as an uneducated rustic youth and worked his way up the ladder. By the time of the Partition, he had become senior supervisor. The highest post an Indian could hold. The Bata shoe factory was his Shangrila. When he left every morning for work in his starched long kurta and jacket, his turban set to an angle, his fierce moustache Simco-waxed and twirled upwards, many a salaam came his way. Lala Deen Dayal was a man to be reckoned with.

Nothing went right for Pitaji when we moved to India. A lot of refugees took their newfound destitution as a challenge and went on to build fortunes for themselves. Pitaji, however, lost the old fire and went about his life apologetically, as if the best was in the past. He tried his hand at many jobs and trades, but none was rewarding. Dispirited and dissatisfied, he became bitterly critical of everything in his adopted land. As his failures increased, so did his wistful recall of the old days in Lahore and the Bata shoe factory.

I remember many an evening spent with my brothers in the tiny living room of our house. We would be sprawled on the red second-hand sofa while Pitaji tuned in to Geetmala, the film music programme on All India Radio.

He'd complain about the poor quality of shoes in India, about how they never fit right, or the leather being rough and the workmanship shoddy.

He would tell everybody and anybody, 'They still owe me a pair of shoes. I hadn't collected my staff quota for the year.'

If only he could get his feet into those genuine Bata Oxfords, he would say time and again. 'How soft the leather, how snug the feel and beautifully balanced the walk. With those shoes on his feet, a man could conquer the world!'

The last few years had been particularly rough on him. He was out of work regularly and he developed chronic sores on his feet. It got so bad that he could hardly walk. For almost a month, he was virtually bedridden. My eldest brother, a doctor, could not figure it out.

'There isn't anything physically wrong with his feet,' he said.

I walked back slowly to my tank. The Bata shoe factory, just a few miles down the road ... What did I want to do? While there had been a great urgency to get out of this place earlier, now I suddenly wanted to be here. I walked towards the colonel's jeep.

'Yes, Captain Dayal?'

'Sir ... I might have made a mistake in my calculations about the fuel. In fact, we may not have enough even to reach our border. But I was thinking ... That factory down the road may have some high speed diesel to run their generators. Maybe they didn't drain it if they left in a hurry?'

'So you're saying let's go up to that factory and take their diesel?'

'Something like that, sir.'

'You do realize that by now that Sabre would have raised a huge stink about us?'

It was a cursory protest. I knew he was keen.

'Maybe we can get in and out before they can react?' I suggested.

'Maybe.' He nodded. 'Mount up, fellows! We are moving ahead!'

I stared at the road ahead. Even with my binoculars, all I could see was the mirage reflected off the hot tarmac road. The Bata shoe factory must lie somewhere in the haze ahead. I felt I was looking at my childhood.

A recce team moved ahead in a jeep. They would be able to give us some advance warning of what lay down the road.

We gave them a few minutes and started off. The earlier chatter and banter had dried up. This was deep enemy territory.

Suddenly, the radio in my tank crackled to life.

'Charger One, three Patton tanks heading your way! Coming down the road,' the look out was yelling.

The Patton tanks outclassed our Shermans in every way. They were bigger, faster and had a more powerful gun. Most importantly, their thicker armour gave them better protection. We needed to come as close as 700 yards to have a chance of destroying a Patton. It could kill us at a distance of 1,300 yards.

People define hell differently. For me hell was those 600 yards, the distance between his kill shot and mine.

My instinct was to turn around and scoot. The best chance of survival was to outrun them. But I had to reach the factory somehow. There had to be a way!

The road on both sides was flanked by tall stalks of sugarcane crop. I ordered my tanks into the dense growth. The fields soon swallowed us. We went in a couple of hundred yards and swung our guns to cover the road.

Almost immediately, we heard the deep roar of their engines. A Patton is an impressive sight. In spite of being shit scared, I couldn't help but admire its feral lines and sleek design. There were three of them speeding down the road to engage our force. They hadn't spotted us.

We'd have to be quick and accurate. They would pass us in seconds.

'Ready. Adjust your sights. Range 400 yards. Wait for it.'

Sweat trickled down and pooled in the narrow of my back, making me shiver.

'Fire!'

Dhani Ram's first shot was a direct hit.

'I've got him, sir!' he yelled.

'Keep on the big bastard till he's finished!'

The loader was a keen lad too. He was tugging the next shell out, pulling the ejection lever on the gun, whipping in a new shell and tapping Dhani Ram in the 'gun ready' signal, all at record speed. Anyway, he couldn't see what I could and the gunner could only see a small part of it. The driver was the guy I felt sorry for. He was squeezed to one side and could only see the stems of sugarcane plants through his aperture. No doubt he was wondering when a shell might head our way.

The first Patton stopped as if it had run into a wall. Its shape seemed to change and like a rubber toy, it collapsed upon itself. Thick smoke poured out of its turret. It was burning from the inside. The other Patton was also on fire from hits by the other tanks.

Our gunners were now peppering the burning tanks with machine gun fire. I saw some movement on one of the stricken tanks.

'Stop firing!' I yelled. 'The crew are bailing out. Let them go.'

I could see them jump off the burning hulls and scurry into the fields, faces bleeding from the metal flakes flying off inside when their tanks had been hit.

It was a courtesy from one tank man to another. I'd heard that in the Second World War, both sides had been guilty of gunning down crew getting out of burning tanks. In our war at least, both sides respected that code.

But in the melee, the third tank had got away. It had disappeared into the cane thickets.

We fired a few rounds into the foliage. It was meant to provoke him and it did. He must have been very young. The Patton came charging out of its hiding place like a wounded rhino.

It was a brave move, but a futile one. There were six guns trained on him. Even so, he caught us by surprise. Our tank was right in his path. Before we could react, he had fired from pointblank range.

He can't miss, was all I had time to think. There was a loud scrapping sound from the side of our turret. The metal walls trembled. A deep dent appeared on the inside, surrounded by a halo of bright singed metal.

'Oh, shit! He's hit us!' our driver screamed. Then there was silence.

I stopped breathing, waiting for the blast wave to cook us to cinder.

But nothing. Nothing at all!

It took a long time for my hands to stop shaking before I could open the hatch and peep out.

The others had blown the Patton to bits. It was ablaze. No one had got out.

How the hell were we alive?

There was a long smear of red hot metal on the side of our tank. His shell had scrapped past without exploding! His barrel had been literally down our throat. Only a miracle could have saved us.

I looked, I mean, really looked at the Shiva calendar for the first time that day.

There was enemy infantry accompanying the Pattons as well. They were engaged by our Jats and firefights were breaking out everywhere.

Just beyond the sugarcane were corn fields. The Pakistani soldiers had taken cover there. We gave a hand to our men by firing red-hot tracer shells into the corn fields. The effect shocked us. The corn, dry and in full yellow ripeness, caught fire. The fields instantly filled up with dense smoke. A lot of the Pakis actually got asphyxiated. It was ghastly. They were getting shot and burnt, but they couldn't retreat and didn't surrender. A few minutes later, all was quiet. The only sound was the crackling of flames from the corn.

The way to the factory was clear. Our narrow escape

was definitely a good sign. Sure, there would be other obstacles, but I knew then that we would be okay.

I had never before acted on instinct alone. The one I had now, to reach that factory, propelled me with a force which was both alien and exhilarating.

We covered the next couple of miles without being attached. The factory suddenly appeared out of the haze. As a factory, it seemed pretty incongruous. Sheds, warehouses, a water tower and offices. What was special for me was that it said rather simply on the large board, 'BATA SHOES'.

Now that I was here, what did I want to do? Pitaji had spoken about this place so often that it had acquired a mythical quality.

The answer struck me as I stepped into one of the warehouses.

By the time I returned, our tanks and jeeps were being refuelled and we had been ordered to return since we were too far for our forces to help us and by now the Pakis would definitely be organizing a counter attack.

A few minutes later, we were speeding back on the G.T. Road and chimera-like, the factory dissolved in the haze.

War is hell, but the truth about it is contradictory. It is grotesque. But it is also beautiful. For all its horror, the awful majesty of combat leaves you dumbstruck. Tracer rounds weaving through the night like shining ribbons, sheets of brilliant metal fire from tanks, glowing phosphorus, the purple–orange panorama of napalm, war machines in battle order. War is terror and despair no doubt, but it's also courage and discovery.

The Geetmala programme on All India Radio is suddenly interrupted by an announcement and an impromptu speech by the prime minister of India, Lal Bahadur Shastri.

The humble voice resonates with earthy determination.

'So, my compatriots, Ayub sahib, the president of Pakistan, has said that in a couple of days, he along with his army will read the namaz at Jama Masjid. I don't know if Ayub sahib is serious, but I thought, why don't we also take a stroll to Lahore. I would like to inform you that units of the Indian Army reached the outskirts of Lahore today morning.'

The phone rings. The old man lifts the receiver and listens intently.

'Thank you, my son,' he whispers.

The old man shrugs off his blanket. His eldest son, the doctor, moves to help him. His father steps down from his bed and settles himself on his trembling, useless feet.

'Pitaji, careful!' the son cries out.

The father brushes his help aside.

He stands shivering and unsteady on his feet.

'I must get up and walk. You see, my shoes are coming.' A smile breaks through the pain. He points at the radio. 'Shastri is right. We must learn to walk again.'

The Contractor

I make my way down the cracked concrete steps to the train platform. The schedule says 6 p.m., but this is eastern UP. They print schedules so the trains can defy them and commuters can eat roasted peanuts off them. The mix of summer heat from the baking fields, diesel smoke and garbage is nauseating. Luckily, I find an empty bench in the shade. I'm early. I take out the rolled up newspaper from my briefcase.

The story on the second page of the suburban edition catches my attention. It's a re-run of an incident that happened in these parts a few months ago. As I read, it all comes back.

Madan Mohan was an agent, a dalal. His job was to work as a cash conduit. Every month he carried cash from a cartel of construction contractors from the neighbouring towns to the Public Works Department offices in Benaras where the cash was distributed to lubricate all kinds of costly government projects. The tenders ran into crores of rupees and the monthly pay offs were in lakhs. Madan Mohan was the courier for ten years.

Then last year, he vanished with the monthly package. After ten years in the business, the fool didn't realize that all construction activity in eastern UP is funded and/or protected by the mafia. They came looking. They knew that Madan Mohan was just a khacharr, a mule, a carrier devoid of brains or guts. They learnt that he had hired a new secretary six months back. Sunita was a beautiful girl and smart. She too had disappeared.

The irony was that this particular shipment of cash had contained marked bills. Sometimes the mafia worked in cahoots with the law to bring down a rival or erring partner. Neither Madan Mohan nor the girl could have known this.

Most of the mafia's menace comes from its reputation of vendetta. It's a reputation that they guard fiercely. Madan Mohan and Sunita were to be hunted down. The next day, the mafia leaked to the press that the stolen money was marked. That ensured that the two could never spend the money. When this article was published, the two were still absconding.

I couldn't help pitying them. Only money can buy you protection and anonymity. Without it, on the run, you're doomed.

There is a rush of activity on the platform. In the haze, I see the form of a diesel locomotive emerge.

From the corner of my eye, I suddenly see her. She's making her way down the footbridge. Anxiously, she looks towards the other end of the platform, expecting to see the train pulling away.

I look at her again. She's beautiful, this woman. Clear skin, a creamy complexion and light eyes. She's not from these parts. Our women are nice, but they're dusky. This one is of the hill people. Garhwal or somewhere beyond. She's wearing a white churidar–kurta and carrying a brown handbag that matches the colour of her hair. She must be around thirty. I look at her hand. No wedding ring.

I know I'm leching, but then, I'm a pro at it. I've got it worked out. I never stay still. Stillness attracts instant attention from the lechee. A good lecher must keep moving his head, shifting position, pretending to do other things.

I don't mind now that the train takes a few more minutes to pull in. She looks at me once, but I've kept my head moving. She's not uncomfortable.

The train arrives, carrying its own smoke and heat to the mix. People surge towards it. This route from Sultanpur to Ballia is a busy one. Ordinary middle-class working folk like me, hurrying to get home or to work. A lot of these men are dressed like me. Most of them are insurance agents, clerks or contractors like me. You may know us from our uniform – safari suit, a couple of pens thrust into the breast pocket and VIP briefcase.

The train starts. She finds a seat at the far end of the compartment. Two safari-suit-clad bhaiyyas push and jostle each other to make room for her. She probably gets that a lot. I don't find any place. I'll go standing. I get that a lot.

She's even lovelier in the dim yellow lighting. She takes out a magazine from her bag. It's a filmy one. That's good. I love films too. Not the kind of mindless nonsense that they're crapping out these days. Nahin yaar, my favourites are the ones from the sixties and seventies. Great romance, beautiful, delicate women, like this one is. Not the muscular bodies with breasts who pass off as heroines these days.

Someone has a radio playing. For the first hour or so, you can still catch the FM station from Sultanpur. They're playing an old Mohammad Rafi song. It's one of my favourites.

Tere mere sapne bas ek rang hain; all our dreams are intertwined, we are one.

She suddenly looks in my direction, aware, I think, that she's being stared at. I pretend to read the railway sign over her head.

I like her, but I know I can never have a woman like her, never know the delight of her love, her body, her caress. We will never be connected. Poets say that to have loved and lost is the greatest pain. Arre nahin bhai, to have never loved at all and have love, pure love as a concept unrequited and trapped inside you, that's the greatest tragedy.

The train pulls into Azamgarh, a suburban stop. Two boys enter and stand at the door. They're talking into cellphones and to each other loudly, abusively. People look away. The train catches speed. The boys decide to move into the compartment. I watch them. They look like trouble. Probably new entrants in a suburban gang, spending their time stealing car stereos, bikes and the like, or involved in petty extortion and turf wars. There are a dozen such gangs in this district, constantly jostling for dominance. Their dark glasses, tight jeans and mannerisms are like a uniform too. And in the end, the uniforms we choose govern our lives, right? They decide our behaviour.

I should have seen it. A pretty girl and two goondatype chokras. It was inevitable. They spot her and nudge one another. The younger one pushes the other forward.

The girl sees them moving towards her. She pretends to focus on the magazine.

In an exaggerated gesture, the first one, the leader, stops before her.

'Oh ho! Arre, look at the chikni.'

'Aaye hai, chikni!'

I look at the passengers sitting next to her. They all look away. It's our suburban mantra: don't get involved.

I hope they move on. They don't. They move closer to her. This is getting out of hand.

'Who are you with, chikni?' the leader asks, looking around.

'What's your name?' the younger one says.

I see her chest heave as she looks around, as if asking for help. None arrives.

'All alone in this bad world? You need someone.' The first one moves close to her.

'Someone like him!' the younger offers.

They laugh.

I can't let this go on. I have to protect her. I can't let them harm her. But like the others, I too am reluctant to move.

Unlike the others, though, I have a connection with this woman. We've exchanged glances. I've fantasized about her over a Rafi song.

Tere mere sapne, the words and the tune seem to get stuck in my head, looping over and over again.

She's mine. Oh, not really. I know I can never be with

her, but in the rule book of incurable romantics, she's mine. Suddenly she looks at me. I'm sure there's an appeal in her eyes.

I move forward, holding onto the seats.

'What are you reading?' the leader asks her.

'Oh! You're looking at Salman Khan! I have a similar body. Wanna see?'

I don't make for an intimidating figure. I know I'm ordinary in every way.

'Let her be, my friend,' I say to him.

He spins around. He was not expecting interference. That's good for me. He's still too young in this game to deal with the unexpected.

'Go away, uncle!' the younger one shouts.

'Haan, go away,' the leader echoes, but I can see the uncertainty in his eyes as they look into mine.

'I will ... If you leave her alone.'

'Why? Who are you? Her brother or her boyfriend?'

'Brother or boyfriend!' The younger one giggles and repeats it like a rhyme.

I've come to diffuse the situation, not escalate it. I don't want to force him to act so as not to lose face.

'I know you're an ustaad, my friend, but let her be. She's not worth the trouble.'

The train is slowing. It's nearing a stop. I realize from the way they're looking out that it's theirs. What a break!

'What kind of trouble?' the leader asks and moves closer.

The train stops. I move up to him and unclasp my

briefcase as if taking out something from it. I hope he falls for it. I look into his eyes.

'The worst kind,' I whisper.

He was expecting something placatory. This throws him.

His friend pulls him away.

'Leave this bhadua, let's go … it's our stop.'

That gives him a way out.

'Yeah, he's her pimp, a bhadua, let's go!'

They get off. I breathe again. The train starts.

I look at the woman. She's smiling. The whole compartment is. I stand next to her with my briefcase. The hero of passenger train 2348 Down!

'Thank you so much,' she says.

'Oh, it was nothing, madam,' I lie.

She smiles again.

Up close, she's even more beautiful. Oh, what's the use, I'll never have her. Although the sidelong glances she's giving me are really flattering. Those two goons had turned out to be very welcome.

'The next stop is mine,' I tell her.

'Oh, mine too.' She's visibly pleased that the hero of the Eastern Railways is getting off with her.

We come out of the station together. It's dark outside. We hesitate, strangers but unwilling just yet to part company.

'Come, I'll walk you home,' I say.

'Thank you, you're very nice.'

'Could be much nicer if given a chance.'

She smiles at that. I feel good when she smiles. I walk

half a step behind her. I study the lovely line of her neck, the arch of her back and the flare of her hips.

Hai, she's beautiful. If only. I sigh.

We come to a middle-income-group apartment block. She stops.

'I don't know how to thank you.'

'I know, a cup of tea will be fine.'

I don't want the meeting to end.

She hesitates, but only for a moment.

'Of course. Let's go up.'

She has a one-bedroom flat on the second floor, no lift. The climb heightens her complexion nicely.

'I'm sure your name is as lovely as you are.'

She blushes at that.

'Sorry. I should have told you earlier. I'm Rati.'

'And I'm Ajay.' I, too, go by many names.

She goes into the kitchen.

I open my briefcase and study the glossy photo of a young woman with fair skin, light eyes and brown hair. It's her all right.

She is back with the tea. It tastes good, spiced with ginger and extra sugar.

'Do you live alone?'

She hesitates before answering.

'Yes, my family lives in Agra.'

'And work?'

'I'm a secretary with a trading company.'

She hasn't got too far.

I take in the small flat, the plastic furniture, the imitation lace curtains.

Without money you can't lie low. You have to move about, find a job. You have to surface.

Poverty can deflate a romance pretty fast. That's why he had been alone when I found him.

She gets up to clear the cups.

She's lovely, this girl, front and back. Pity we can't be together, can't fall in love.

Tere mere sapne starts playing in my head.

I smother it. This is the time I let the coldness in. It's a technique to get ... detached.

When she returns, I have my briefcase open. I am looking at the photo again and my hand is on the revolver inside. The steel feels colder today.

It's an old gun, unmarked and untraceable. The silencer is of my own design. Simple steel tube, perforated and held by flex wire. Good for only two shots. But that's all I ever need. None of this stuff can ever be traced back to me.

I call her by her name, her real name. It's always the final check.

'Really, Sunita, did you actually think you could get away?'

Her eyes go wide.

I take out the gun.

I watch her eyes. Just for a second, I'm able to peep into her soul.

Tere mere sapne plays again. I see a connection in that final moment before I pull the trigger, before the thunder.

People say the act of killing is a lonely one. Not for me. It's the only time I've been able to make connections, intimate ones.

I told you I was a contractor. And she was my contract.

A Sound Idea

There are those who are born and bred in big cities and then there are the outsiders. The outsiders can't understand how we city dwellers take the stress, the noise, the overcrowding. Why we need the over-stimulation or why we feel isolated and get bored so easily. The gasoline fumes blended with hot stale air from a million air-conditioning vents gives all us inmates a constant hang-dog expression. And yes, to an outsider we're all inmates of this urban prison. Morning to night, rain or shine, like terriers we keep searching, sniffing, pawing, crawling and chasing elusive bones. And then, for a few hours, we come home.

It takes an outsider to point out that the tiny hovels we happily call home are not much bigger than a zoo cage. For me, the outsider that shone the light was my wife. She'd lived all her life with her parents in suburban Pune, miles from the big city of Mumbai. Daddy's double-storeyed bungalow had views that most of us in Mumbai can only enjoy in movies or paintings: a lawn and a backyard.

To be fair to her, she was graceful enough to wait a week after our wedding before using words like dump and slum for my one-bedroom flat.

Any middle-class bloke from a big city will tell you that just owning a couple of walls to hold a roof over your head is an achievement. So you can imagine my state when my wife of a few days started talking about houses with gardens front and back!

A sound engineer's existence is at best middle-class, unless he finds that 'special' tune and cracks the cut-throat market. That tune had eluded me so far. Have you noticed though, that once wives convince themselves that something can be acquired, they immediately discard all reality. My wife was convinced that if I looked hard enough, I would find a house like she wanted. The belief was flattering and infuriating at the same time.

Don't get me wrong. I love my wife. Leena's a doll. She's got more beauty and brains than all my friends' wives' put together. And she knows it.

God save us from women who know their value!

Sometimes I wonder why she chose me. I'm all right, I guess, but I'm no catch. We had a whirlwind courtship, I clenched my belly and popped the question, and she said yes!

Among Leena's many interests was astrology. She picked out an auspicious date. Her parents were abroad at that time, so we decided to have a court marriage. We're still to have the big reception and I am yet to make a formal trip to meet the in-laws.

It was only a matter of time before she had me scouting in earnest for 'livable' places.

For some time, she almost made me believe that it was possible. But the reality was that after scraping the bottom of my financial barrel and borrowing from everyone I knew, I couldn't manage more than thirty lakh rupees. That's like spare change in the highly inflated real estate market.

Strangely enough, my wife's belief in our ability to find her dream house turned out to be pretty accurate. It was not an ordinary flat that we found, but a cottage with stucco-finish walls and a sloping Mediterranean roof. A cottage smack in the middle of the city, enclosed in its personal little grove of mango trees. The baroque-style fountain and pristine white marble flooring in the living room were a bit much. Okay, I'm from the big slummy city, I have no taste. But for Leena, it was out of a fairy tale. 'It's so much like Daddy's' were high words of praise for me.

Every fairy tale must have its goblin, and for the cottage, it was the real estate agent, Mishra.

'Don't worry, darling,' said Leena. 'Nothing so dreamy ever comes unattached.'

Funny, she's never said anything like that about me.

Mishra is a hard nut to crack. Even though the cottage has been lying vacant for years, he's in no hurry to sell.

'Arre, Mukul sahib, I've waited so many years, I'll wait some more. The owners live abroad. The prices will pick up in a year or so. My best price is eighty-five lakhs. No negotiations, huh. Please.'

Over four months I have tried cultivating the man, but Mishra, with his betel-juice-stained, starched kurtas and quivering belly, never gets ruffled.

One evening, I had just finished a long recording session at my studio and was lighting up a cigarette before locking up. Can't smoke at home, you know, Leena doesn't approve. A man walked into the studio. He was an agent for a new stereo manufacturer. We get a lot of walk-in salesmen from new sound companies and I try to shoo him out. This one is more adamant than the rest.

He says his company is offering something revolutionary in sound technology. He takes out of his bag three speakers the size of golf balls, a woofer the size of a cigarette packet and a remote control.

When he hits the play button, the sound is unmatched for in depth and quality. Much larger and more elaborate sound systems don't produce the same effect. I'm impressed.

'In fact, sir, you can use it for all your live background sound playbacks. The quality of sound is crystal clear, but the real speciality of the system is its remote. It's got a range of 200 metres.'

I set up the system and check it out. The guy is right. The sound is great and the remote works even from across the street.

'I like it, but five lakhs is too much for this.'

'Sir, you don't have to pay now. Just keep it, try it out for fifteen days. Give me a post-dated cheque. I'll encash it only after two weeks. But I know you'll never want to give it back.'

That night, long after Leena has fallen asleep, I make myself some tea and creep out to the balcony for a smoke. At first, the idea appears just as a niggling thought, like you've missed something in the picture. Before long, I've smoked half the packet. Then suddenly it's upon me with heart-pounding clarity.

The sky has just started turning a shade lighter. I want to go in and wake Leena.

But I don't have to. I know that she's there behind me on the balcony. I haven't seen her, but I've always been able to sense her presence. I've seen her many times like this, just standing there looking at me. It's flattering mostly, but sometimes it gives me a start. The overcast pre-monsoon sky discharges a few drops.

I take her back into the flat to tell her my idea.

'Sweetheart, why do you think that though the cottage is so beautiful, it's priced only at eighty-five lakhs? I mean, a place like that, in Mumbai, should be worth much more,' I tell her.

'I don't know. Maybe it's isolated, or the access road is bad. I never thought about it. Maybe you big-city types are only happy when you live nose to armpit!'

Wow! It's 4 a.m. and she can still be testy.

'I'll tell you what I think. Nobody says this openly, but I think it's because the right boundary wall of the cottage is adjacent to an old deserted cemetery.'

'Really? I had no idea.' Leena seems a little disturbed.

'Hey, how does it matter, right? I mean, for us it's our dream house.'

'You're right. I don't care. That place is too pretty for me to care.'

This was the time to reveal my master plan. I wanted to make it sound just right.

'You and I don't care, my darling, but people do. People are superstitious, you know. You'd think only illiterate rural bumpkins would be that way, but people in cities are no different. Deep inside, everybody has this dread of the supernatural. Nobody's comfortable living next to an old graveyard. I think that's the real reason not many people are interested in the place.'

I give her my best conspiratorial smile.

'Now listen, till now there is only an abstract fear because of the proximity of the house to the graveyard. What if this fear becomes real?'

'Meaning?'

'Meaning, what if something actually happens that shows people that there is something weird about this place?'

'What do you mean, weird?'

'You know, what if this place were haunted? People would get scared out of their wits. Even those who show a minor interest will be put off. Then that Mishra is cornered. You're an economics graduate. You know what happens when there's only one buyer. He dictates the price!'

Leena is a smart woman, but I don't blame her for not following. It takes a particularly unscrupulous bent of mind to understand what I was plotting.

I am big-city born and bred. You don't make it here without jimmying ethics a little.

'I don't get it. Why are you telling me all this? Nothing like that ... that weirdness has happened. Has it?'

'No, it hasn't, darling, but it can be made to happen.' I use my smile again.

'Made to happen? How?'

I tell her about the salesman and the new sound system. I tell her about its incredibly small size, the depth of its sound and the range of its remote control. How easy it would be to set up the system in the cemetery one night and play some bloodcurdling sounds. He had access to hundreds of recordings. They could then count on the story to spread till that little cottage became a complete pariah.

'I know it sounds risky, sweetie, but I know it can work, and remember the saying – desperate times need desperate measures.'

I have to say this about Leena. She didn't hesitate for even a minute. Whatever misgivings she might have had, ethical or otherwise, were eroded by the misery of our cramped one-bedroom existence.

'How do we pull it off?' That's all she asked.

'We'll get that system. Then one evening we'll go and rig the speakers on a tree in the cemetery ... They're too small to be noticed. After that, all we do is park some distance away and play our concert! It'll be our own private sting operation!'

Her eyes turn smoky with promise as she leans closer and whispers in my ear.

'I'd love that. Our own private sting.'

The next day I call the salesman and ask him to deliver the sound system. The deal is that he will only deposit my cheque fifteen days later. That evening, Leena and I drive past the cottage and park near the cemetery. There's no one around. This place has been deserted for years. Most of the graves have been overrun by the undergrowth.

I spot a tree with a wide fork in the middle.

'That's the one.' I point and Leena nods.

It's still light, but the place makes us uncomfortable. We don't stay a moment longer than necessary.

Over the next two days I put aside all other work. I go through the hundreds of recordings in my data bank. It's difficult to find a sound that is scary yet subtle.

On the second evening, I finally find it. It's a background score from an old movie that had got shelved. It's the sound of a woman. A stifled shriek followed by heavy raspy breathing. But the crowning feature is the very real rustling of cloth at the end of the track. Just listening to that sound, even in the studio, makes me uneasy. I remember the words of an old sound engineer I had started as an apprentice with:

'Sound is the most effective medium, Mukul. Far more impactful than words or images. You know, the brain retains more sounds than images. Always remember that when your clients are being difficult.'

The old boy was absolutely right.

In the evening I open a bottle of wine and play Leena's favourite Michael Buble CD.

'If we play this recording one night and then again after a couple of nights, people who hear it will be convinced that there is something strange about the cemetery. I can see it all happening. We will finally have a house, darling. A real house with a garden. A place to bring up kids in. Maybe even a private studio. Waah! What a life it'll be!'

Finally our big night arrives. Just past midnight, Leena and I park our car a couple of hundred metres from the cemetery. Leena holds a flashlight as I climb the tree we had marked out earlier and install the micro speakers, the woofer and a battery pack.

Through the dense undergrowth some lights can be seen across a stretch of open ground.

'See that, honey,' I tell Leena, 'There's a new building site. Quite a few construction workers stay overnight in these sites. They'll be our front-row audience.'

We're both breathing hard from the excitement.

Back in the car, when we hit 'play' on the remote, the effect is startling. In this dark and foreboding landscape, the sound from those speakers is hair-raising.

Leena shivers and snuggles closer to me.

'How will we know that the plan is working?' she asks.

'I've thought about that. I know this guy, Raju. He's that estate agent Mishra's office boy. I've been cultivating him for some time ... You know, ten bucks now and then. He'll report back to me directly from Mishra's office. But I think we may need to play this a few times.'

'I'm not going back there again.' She shivers again.

'Hey, sweetheart, how can you be scared of your own creation? Think of the payback. Focus on that.'

A few days later, we repeat our performance.

What we didn't know then was that our first 'show' hadn't gone unnoticed. Some workers had heard the sounds and the first buzz had already begun. After the second time, people started getting convinced that all was not right with that graveyard. Soon the grapevine was aflame with stories of ghosts and spirits. The more imaginative even claimed sightings.

'Look at these people! I've even heard stories of

frightening cries and tortured screams being heard. Let them add more spice ... Good for us!' I tell Leena.

Although Mishra is full of bluster and confidence, unknown to us, the cottage has been a thorn in his side for a long time. He's scared that if the press gets wind of the haunted graveyard story, that's the end of the sale.

It's not long before I get a call from him.

I turn around. I can sense that Leena's been standing behind me the whole time.

'He's brought the price down to fifty lakh. We just have to wait. He'll come around to our budget.'

'Wow! Our dream house. You're so smart! I've married a genius!'

I'll lap up whatever words of praise come my way. God knows they're few and far between!

The only other time I saw her this ecstatic was when I gifted her a Mughal miniature painting. It cost a couple of months' pay, but the look on her face was worth it. She can spend hours with stuff like that.

'Mukul, let's not wait. I'll arrange for the rest of the money through a bank loan. This house is too good to take a chance with.'

I tell her that banks right now are being hugely anal about who they give loans to.

'Don't worry about it. A close college friend is the head of a bank. He'll do it.'

I'm a little surprised. Like a lot of great looking women, Leena is mostly wary of the intentions of men.

'No free lunches with men' is something I've heard very often. This house must be really important to her.

The next day I go to Mishra's office and pay him a deposit of two lakh for the house.

The day after that, the story about the haunted graveyard hits the stands.

A few days later, I get a call from Mishra's office. I wink at Raju, my office boy contact, before walking in. There are some people in his office. The presence that dominates the whole room is a man of about sixty. He's tall and lean with a beaked nose and the sharpest piercing eyes I've ever seen. His silver-grey hair is swept back in a ponytail. A profusion of rings with coloured stones on his fingers catches the light. There is a strange mystical aura about him. He's flanked on both sides by assistants.

Mishra gets up as I enter.

'Hi, Mukul. This is Professor Jai Varma.'

I extend my hand, but there's no response from the mystery man.

'Professor sahib called me yesterday. You see, he's very interested in that cottage. He has offered eighty-five lakh, my original price. Since we haven't signed a deal yet, I'll just return your deposit.' He takes the money out of the drawer.

I'm not sure what the hell is going on. This has got to be the shortest-lived euphoria ever.

I turn to the professor.

'But haven't you heard about the place? Has he told you about it, sir?'

'Arre, that is why professor sahib is interested. He's doing some research.'

'Research? What research?'

The professor gives me a penetrating look once over. He speaks in a fruity baritone.

'He's right. I'm a professor of occultology. It's the study of occult practices and supernatural phenomena or apparitions and ghosts as you lay people call them. I've been working in the United States for the past ten years. My area of expertise is the tracking of supernatural energy or spirits, as you call them. I specialize in feminine spirits.'

He sizes me up, probably to see if I'm worthy of more information. Apparently I am.

'Humeira was a beautiful lady of the Mughal court who lived in the sixteenth century. She was known for her looks and even more, for her virtue. She'd never lifted her veil to any man except her husband. The emperor of that time, Shah Jahan, built a canopied market called the Meena Bazar. It was a market for the court, with lavish stalls and silks and jewels from all over the world. Actually it was an elaborate pantomime. The shops were run by the court ladies who haggled over prices, joshed each other in a flirtatious, mildly bacchanalian fiesta. Freely dispensed spiced wine helped loosen the rigid social lines. It was all a bit of a sexual tease. The only place where, by the emperor's decree, all the court ladies had to wear veils made of only gossamer-thin muslin.'

The professor stops to take a sip of the steaming tea which had been brought in. He seems to slurp the tea, but I can tell what he really relishes is the tale.

'Nobody, not even the emperor, could have realized the effect of such permissiveness.

'A senior Amir caught a glimpse of Humeira and was bewitched by her beauty. He was ready to barter anything to possess her. He was a powerful man. Humeira's husband worked under him. The Amir owned an elegant palace made of pristine makrana marble. Made by a Turkish architect, it was the first of its kind.

'Humeira and her husband were Persian immigrants. Though her husband was employed as a high official in the Mughal court, he was constantly jockeying to rid himself of the 'outsider' badge. In those days, status was totally derived from land and property. Ownership of a rare makrana palace would no doubt provide an instant fillip to his status.

'Humeira, meanwhile, had remained a simple girl who found it difficult to adjust to the jealousies of the upper-class zenana and the intrigues of Hindustani society. She had become a liability. Her husband, on the other hand, had found his true calling amidst the politics and bluster of the Mughal court. It was essential for an officer to have a patron to advance his career and counter the intrigues of his rivals. Her husband saw a double benefit. He offered her to his elderly overlord in exchange for the marble palace and his patronage. She would never have agreed willingly, so the husband pretended that he was divorcing her for another.

'But the emperor found out and was livid at the level of depravity of his courtiers. Humeira was betrayed and killed by her husband and her lover so that she couldn't give evidence against them. They chose a particularly malevolent method.

'She celebrated her husband's birthday each year with a garden party. In the fall, the high wind with the first hint of a chill had blown dry leaves in heaps all over the garden. They poisoned her and hid her body beneath a bed of dry leaves. The next day the heaps of leaves were burnt.'

The professor looks at me.

'Do you see? Not only did they murder her for their individual lust, but they even denied her a proper burial. Her spirit has been coming back over the centuries, but this is the first reported contact in the last fifty years.'

I can only stare at the man.

'But how will you find it? And what will you do with it?'

He smiles patiently.

'It's too complicated. You won't understand it. We use sophisticated technology like lasers and sonar and computers.'

This is getting crazy!

'What is it? Is it a ghost? Why does it come back?'

'Oh, the legend is that Humeira was killed by the sting of a kazdum, Persian for scorpion. Persian was the language of the Mughal nobles. Kazdum means poisoned tail. In Persia, the scorpion was despised not only for its sting, but also because there was poison in its heart, in its intent.

'She always comes back to places infested by scorpions, like the cemetery is. Death follows in her wake and her victims have always been men.'

'But how do you know it's her?' I ask.

'Oh, that's simple. Because of the sound. The reported

sound is a dead giveaway. It's the exact same sound of Humeira.'

This is fast spinning out of control. I am starting to get desperate now.

'But, sir, you haven't seen or heard anything yourself, have you? You're just going by rumours. You know how fickle Indians can be when talking about ghosts and all.'

The professor's eyes flash and his voice turns cold.

'That's the problem with you young people. Indians are this and that ... Everything Western is right. My friend, we have an ancient and knowledgeable culture. We were investigating the supernatural long before the West had any idea about it.

'You want to know how I know it's the same spirit? I'll tell you. It's because of the sound. Yes, the rustling of cloth at the end. That's the key, the telltale sign of Humeira.

'Her dying shriek is always followed by the sound of her coming back to retrieve her veil, the sign of her purity. It's the veil that trails and rubs on dry leaves as she leaves her body.'

This is insane. I want to shout out the truth to this mad man.

'I need the house because it's the perfect vantage point to set-up our equipment. It might take time, but I can wait. I know that she'll be back. My research is funded by an American foundation. Money does not matter. You can never match us. Get yourself some other place.'

I hear the phone ring before I enter my flat. My expression must be a giveaway because it knocks Leena's smile right off. I move to pick up the phone.

'Morning, Mr Mukul, Just wanted to tell you that we encashed your cheque today since the two weeks are up. Thanks, it was great doing business with you.'

I stare dumbly at the handset. Five lakhs for the stereo system down the drain and no house to show for it.

Then I hear the lilting jingle of my cellphone.

It's the same deep baritone I've grown to hate. The tone of the professor's voice is softer now, almost civil.

'I found some of your stuff on my property. You know, the things you planted on a tree. I just came to know that you're a sound engineer. I have the equipment, my friend, all I need now is the sound. You have it, don't you? I'm sure we can work out a deal. As I explained earlier, the grant for my research depends on it.'

I take a couple of deep breaths.

'I get it, professor. I have what you need, sir. My offer is this: pay for half the cost of the house, it'll be in my name and I'll live in it with my wife. We'll let you keep your gadgets there to keep the pretence of your research going and I'll give you a copy of my recording.'

I can tell from his silence that he is going to agree to my proposal. Gone is the attitude, gone the crappy spirit of scientific enquiry and gone the saga of some ancient damsel. This is a deal in the real world, something I can understand. He doesn't have a choice really. He is paying for my silence. Sometimes silence is really the best sound.

The arrangement works out just fine. We move into our cottage. The professor takes the outhouse and parks his equipment there, milking the American grant for all it's worth. Leena and the professor hit it off really well.

Probably because of their common interests in astrology, the occult and the like. I can just about tolerate him. There are aspects to the man that I just can't understand. I'm not kicked that Leena has started spending time with him, but I don't want to sound like a typical husband about it.

A few days later, I've just about locked up my studio. The monsoon has burst upon the city in full fury. The first few days are always bad. The waterlogging and traffic snarls are a nightmare. I'm not looking forward to the drive. The house deal has left me with some extra cash and I've just got myself a new SUV. That baby should be good at handling slippery roads.

A couple of hundred metres and I'm stuck in a long line of cars crawling forward.

Above the thwack of the windshield wipers I hear my cellphone ring.

It's the agent from the stereo company.

'Mr Mukul, sir, I'm really sorry, but there's been a bad mistake by us. Our head office called from Singapore. They accidentally packed the wrong remote controls in this lot. You must be wondering why yours are not working. Actually everyone else we sold it to has called us. Maybe you didn't try out the remote. I called to say we'll change it by next week.'

'How can that be? Mine worked.'

'Not possible, sir. The frequencies don't match.'

What the hell is going on?

There is something very weird happening here. My remote control has played not once in that cemetery, but twice.

I don't know why, but I think it's got something to do with the professor. I always suspected him.

Oh, God! Leena is alone in the house right now with him. In my rush, I dial a wrong number twice. The phone is in the kitchen. I can hear it ring in that empty way when you know nobody's there. I try her cell. No reply there either. Where the hell is she? What has happened?

What has he done to her?

Should I call the cops? But what will I tell them?

Why did I leave her with that maniac?

The traffic ahead inches forward. I hit the horn continuously. I try to distract myself by switching FM channels on the radio.

The rain is coming down in sheets now.

The road ahead is slick with wet mud. If I stay on this main road I'll probably take more than an hour to get home. Just ahead, I see a turn, it's an arterial road that looks a little slushy because of the rain. But it'll cut the driving time by half, plus I'd skip the traffic.

My new SUV should be able to handle it. Didn't they advertise it as a great off-road drive?

Why isn't she answering the phone?

As I turn to take the side road, my car skids a little on the slick surface. It's getting dark and I need my headlights on the unlit road.

A thought comes to me. This road runs through the entire length of the cemetery to get to our house.

The heavy rain has reduced the road to little more than a mud track. The heavy SUV skids again. I fight the wheel and the tyres swing back under control.

I begin to regret a few decisions. Like taking this road … like leaving Leena alone … like getting involved in the matter of this house.

What the hell! It wasn't really my fault.

She wanted the house. Come to think of it, she forced me to look for a new house.

And *this* house. I remember her waving a newspaper ad … She'd found it.

She got the loan organized for it. I didn't even ask how.

Why had I never met any of her friends? Even her parents, including her dear 'Daddy'?

'Oh! You'll soon get to meet everybody, darling.'

When I was hesitant to make a deal with the crazy professor, she was the one who pushed me.

I wrench the wheel hard to prevent another skid. It's really coming down. I can barely see the road.

And now this interest in that madman's work?

I had asked her if she was uncomfortable when she was alone so close to a cemetery.

'No, I find it very … *restful,*' she'd said.

The radio has all this time been playing the latest film songs. A new programme entertaining requests has just begun. They're playing songs for people by their sunsigns.

The volume suddenly jumps a couple of notches. They're interviewing some hotshot astrologer between songs. His voice is clear.

'This one goes out to all those born in October and November. The sign of the Scorpio, known as Serket to the Egyptians and Kazdum to the Persians.'

Kazdum ... kazdum ... where have I heard this word before?

Humeira was killed by the sting of a kazdum, Persian for scorpion.

Her victims have always been men.

The whole car is shuddering now. I don't know if I'm on the road or if there is a road left at all.

I remember her fascination for that Mughal painting. The scene of a celeberation.

'We'll celebrate the twenty-ninth of October in our new house, my darling. We'll call all our friends. It'll be a birthday you'll remember.'

I remember the profusion of rings on the professor's hands.

'Oh, those are for my sunsign.' He smiled. 'Like you, I'm also a scorpio.'

Kazdum is not Persian for scorpion alone. It's also Scorpio the sunsign. I want to shout it out to the professor now.

The radio breaks in. 'The whole programme today is for Scorpios. An interesting fact, guys. Did you know that according to a poll, Mumbai has the highest number of people with the Scorpio sunsigns in the country?'

Every century she visits a place infested with scorpions.

I grab my cellphone. I have to warn him.

It's a miracle I can dial in the badly jostling vehicle.

The phone rings endlessly. It's too late.

I can see the lights of our house in the distance. Through the rain, they seem blurred. I can't judge the distance. They may be miles away or just around the next bend.

Where is she?

I don't have to look in the rearview mirror. I know who's in the back seat. I told you, I can always sense her presence.

Any sound I might have made has dried in my throat, an urgent high-pitched scream fills my world. It seems to come from the speakers, from outside, from everywhere. In spite of my state, I smile. I recognize it. It's my own recording.

I look in the mirror.

I can't see her face. It's difficult to make out through the heavy veil she's wearing.

The car lurches and goes into a skid.

The tyres screech to find traction. The car seems to be lifted off the ground and carried in a river of mud.

This time I know it's futile to fight.

Betrayal

The party was a success.

It was the launch of Preeti's new bestseller, the eighth one in a row, and the speaker had worked himself into a state.

'Preeti Mishra is not just an author, she's not even a person. She's a concept. Her books are magical tales of passion. Even her critics can't deny that her stories have helped hundreds of women become comfortable with their own sexuality. As soon as she spins a new story, it's lapped up by her adoring readership – thousands of lovelorn women who are starved of passion in their bedrooms and their lives.'

Jerk! Preeti almost said it aloud. She had heard other wives say this about their husbands all the time, but seldom did they mean it with such intensity.

Anil, oblivious to her thoughts, continued, 'And doesn't it look like she's stepped out of one of her own novels? Demure and pretty. Sexy, yes, but classy ... something women have forgotten to be. Over the years many have tried to emulate her, but I know that imagination,' he almost leered, 'and it cannot be imitated.'

She escaped to the bar. The speech was short, thankfully. Look at him now. Making the right moves, a nod here, a smile there. He had always been more business manager than husband. And there in the corner was Anita, chatting with her publisher, the self-assured smile firmly in place. Anita, two years older than her. Two years the world would never let her forget. Parents, relatives, friends: 'Listen to Anita. She's your elder sister.' Anita, always the leader, the performer. Popular and smug. She had always ridiculed Preeti's attempts at writing and in the early days it had been tough. Nobody wanted to look at her work.

But success, when it had come, was like a dam burst, flooding them all.

Preeti could almost hear Anita cracking some new deal with her publisher. It had started with occasional weekend advice as Anita did not have much time to spare from her busy practice. Till the workload increased and Anita started looking after her finances exclusively.

How that must have hurt her! Working for little Preeti. But Anita shifted gears smoothly, without a hint of sibling rivalry. She had always been smart and now she was in command. Pretending that the writing was secondary, as if the main thing was looking after the money.

But what they all didn't know was that the money might stop coming in. Her publisher had warned her that sales were falling. A dozen bestsellers and three major film scripts behind her and they worried about a miniscule dip in the sales graph. The public was tiring of the same stuff. Maybe something with an edge, they said. Really, what was more edgy than her brand of erotic fiction.

'A new world of evocative risk taking.' Isn't that what the critics had said of her last book? They wanted edgier than that? People wanted something different to slake their jaded appetites. But people, people were sheep, weren't they?

She could sense impending failure. It seemed to move about in the room amidst the champagne and the hors d'oeuvres. What if the magic dried up? The dream she had been living the last few years could be over ... soon. She had got used to all this – the ritzy lifestyle, the role of the pampered celebrity. But the drop would be a long and painful one. They never dropped you cold. Tabloids would ease her out from page three centre to a couple of lines on the last page, to fortnightly mentions to oblivion. Each kick down discussed and dissected for the entertainment of all.

Sometimes she thought her twin's life was better. Pari, her twin sister, was deaf and mute, comfortably cocooned from all the world. She was lucky, she didn't have to kowtow to anyone. The price she had to pay was terrible, of course. She had been looked down upon and ignored all her life for her horrible handicap. But Preeti had sworn to look after her. Even now Pari was dependent on her for all her physical needs and she was the only one Pari would freely communicate with.

And if Anita was contemptuous towards Preeti, she abhorred the very existence of Pari. She remembered a conversation she had overheard between Anita and her husband Anil some time back.

'She's always so protective about that Pari. I just can't stand that ...' Anita's impatient tone was hushed.

'I know, Anita, but she is just a ...'

'I know it's unreasonable to hate that inanimate ...'

'Who named her?' he asked.

'Oh, Preeti ... who else! When she came home with mother, nobody called her anything for a long time till Preeti started calling her Pari ... a fairy ... huh!'

'And the burning incident?' Anil asked.

'It was an accident. We were just kids. I know Preeti believes that it was deliberate, but it wasn't.'

'The marks on her ... have they been there since then?'

'Yeah, they have, but I don't understand ... I mean what's the big deal. She should have been got rid off a long time back.'

'Got rid off!' The words screamed in Preeti's head. Just because Pari was handicapped and defenseless, did they think she was also brain dead? If they only knew what a lively mind the poor 'dumb' waif had.

Suddenly she'd had enough of the party, the booze-soaked crowd, the organized rapture. She went up to Pari and took her hand. Their communication was so perfect that she did not need to speak. Nobody noticed them heading for the door.

She caught a glimpse of Anil getting a drink for Anita. They stood there talking, smiling, almost caressing, she imagined. She turned to Pari and saw that Pari had noticed it too. She saw the bright piercing look come upon her twin's face and knew that Pari was ready to speak.

In this state of excitement, Pari was unrestrained in her speech. Of course, to an outsider, their exchange would be meaningless. Not that anyone would really witness such a conversation – Pari insisted on communicating only in private. Even then, they used a mix of sign language and a sort of plugged in telepathy.

Pari's next words gushed out staccato.

'Newspaper headlines in a few months will read: "Famous author's husband dead, suspected murder ... investigation begins."'

'Wait, let me get this. Go slow. Is this a new story idea coming?' Preeti asked.

But Pari was brusque.

'Yes, it is ... or may be more than just a story. Don't interrupt me, it ruins the flow.' Pari made the sign for impatience.

'One evening the police will respond to a hysterical call from a suburban home. They will find Anil at the bottom of the stairs ... dead.'

'Whoa! Did you say Anil?'

Preeti couldn't help interjecting.

'Shhh ...' Pari hissed. 'Don't interrupt me again or I'll go silent.'

'No, sorry. I just thought you said Anil.'

Preeti remembered a time when Pari, pissed off at something, had gone 'silent'. Sick with worry, Preeti had not been able to pen a single thought during that time. It seemed her writing had soured.

'Yes, I said Anil. ANIL ... your husband. You had better listen carefully, love. Your future – no, our future depends on it.'

The resolve in Pari's eyes was terrifying, but Preeti had seen it before. It was there whenever Pari perceived any threat to their future. She looked fondly at Pari and thought, she's really concerned about me ... has always been. She's my guardian and muse.

But deep down, she knew that Pari had been much more than just an inspiration for her work, and her great concern for Preeti's future was also because it was inextricably connected to her own.

'So,' Pari continued, 'Anil's body is found at the bottom of the staircase. You will automatically become the main suspect, as spouses do. But surprisingly, no motive. Find the motive and find the killer – that's how cops work. In your case, no motive.'

'My case!' It came out as a shout. Preeti also noticed that Pari had dropped the third person reference and was addressing her directly.

'Yes, Larla, your case.' Pari used their childhood endearment. 'Your case, you poor, pathetic girl. And if you don't do as I say, you're finished and so am I and that I will not let happen. Your popularity is at an all-time low, something has to be done, and drastic times ... you know the saying.'

'But Pari, what you're suggesting is murder!'

'Yes, I am! And if you'd listened to me earlier it wouldn't have come to this. I've been telling you for the longest time that this erotica nonsense is getting outdated, haven't I? But, no, you wouldn't listen ... Please, Pari, give me one more story ... just one more ... please. So now, you will do as I say and the story that I give you will save you and us from extinction.'

Preeti was getting scared. Pari in this defender of 'home turf' role had always been terrifying, but murder?

When Pari got this way she was unstoppable and that was ... scary!

'Let me just appraise you of your situation,' Pari continued. 'In case, knowing your huge capacity for self-delusion, you've forgotten the past.

'A shy, introverted girl, easily intimidated by everyone – parents, friends and especially an older sister. A sister who was the opposite – smart and outgoing, the one everyone has an eye on. "Watch her, she'll become something someday." And the younger one just doesn't measure up. She's not particularly good at anything. Her only real companion is her deaf–mute twin. A loner, she stays lost in her dreams which spin into tales she wants to put on paper. Do you remember the rejections? She starts writing erotic fiction and discovers accidentally that her twin has quite a flair for it. Suddenly, she's a huge success. Her wildest dreams have come true. And her elder sister, that hateful monstrosity now comes to work for her. Wasn't that the best?'

'Yes ... it was ... the best.' Preeti remembered all the childhood cruelties.

'So, tell me, where would we be if the security of all this success is taken away. What would you be left with, baby? A marriage without any depth. Anita, who you've hated your entire life. These people are expendable. What is not is your future. And your life is only about writing and through you, so is mine. You must have a bestseller, a story beyond all else. "Something edgy," your publisher said. We'll give them betrayal, the most sizzling ingredient of art and of the daily news. It's easily understood by bodies and souls, whether they reside in back alleys, suburbs or pent houses.'

Preeti looked into Pari's eyes. They blazed with the deepest, wildest fury Preeti had ever seen. She suddenly realized with a start that her twin was mad enough to murder or at least plan it. And she knew that just like everything else, it was only a matter of time before she let herself be persuaded by Pari. If Pari was a little crazy, then the craziness was infectious, for Preeti felt it too, as also a tremendous sense of release now that Pari had taken charge.

'Listen, in this case, art will follow real life. These incidents in the story I'm telling you will have already happened or been made to happen in your life. The book that follows will be a gritty real-life account.

'You will make a model grieving widow. A very unlikely candidate for such a heinous act and also, you have no motive – you have the money, he has none. He works for you, in fact. He's not a particularly attractive man. No hint of another woman. No motive for the police to follow. What do they do? The case is highly publicized, they have to come up with something. So they will put one of their ace investigators on the job. Investigators become good not because of any outstanding intuitive skills or any other Sherlock-like ways. They are just more patient than others and are dogged in their ...'

'Research.' Preeti finished for her.

Pari was grinning. 'The Super,' she said.

'The Super.' Preeti agreed. She remembered him from many years ago, looking dashing in his uniform. 'Super' she used to call him, a superintendent in the police force. She'd even modelled one of her novel's heroes after him. Pari was quoting him now.

'So research they will. They'll dig into everybody's background and find that our elder sister, Anita, is something of an enigma. A willful, strong personality, egoistic, yet working for you. They'll find that her independent C.A. practice has, in fact, been floundering. When she came to work for you, she did not have many better options. They'll come to know that Anita and Anil were close, but how close? They had plenty of opportunities to be together when they travelled for book fairs and literary festivals, didn't they?'

Preeti nodded. She was mesmerized by Pari's storytelling technique, as always. This would have been just one more of her stories but for the menace in her narration. But if this plot went wrong, she couldn't simply hit delete and rewrite the climax. She found the finality of it exciting. They settled down on their favourite couch and carried on long into the night.

It went exactly as Pari had forecast. Almost as if she had stage managed this evil opera. Like Pari had predicted, however, she felt no remorse.

The police, sometimes she had to stop from laughing aloud, had been childishly predictable. They had put one of their crack detectives on the case, a Chief Inspector S.K. Patil. This gentleman had gone and faithfully reconstructed the case that Pari had planted for him, without missing a beat.

But when they came to arrest Anita – that was a glorious

moment – any qualms Preeti might have had faded. Anita had to be physically restrained and was hysterically screaming her innocence while being taken away.

Chief Patil was a large man with a smoker's noisy breathing. He had come up to Preeti in his sombre manner to console her. 'I know how devastating it must be, ma'am, first to cope with your husband's tragic demise and now your sister's act of ...'

'Betrayal,' she supplied the word. He nodded.

She was thankful for the sedative they had automatically administered. Without it, she would not have been able to control the waves of wild, elated laughter that rose in her. She had asked Patil in a choked voice, 'What happened, Inspector? It's all so confusing for me.'

Patil looked at her with what could only have been pity before replying.

'I'm sorry, but your husband was having an affair with your sister, and he threatened to tell you,' he blurted out.

'I think that your husband wanted to come clean. He was basically a ... moral man.'

She saw him hesitate and thought, I think he wants to say weak and I agree. Anil was just too scared, too weak to rock the boat. To even contemplate cheating on me.

'Anita knew that if Anil came to you with this, you might eventually forgive him, but for Anita, it was over. She must have known that you would ...'

'I could never forgive her ...' Preeti managed to gasp convincingly. 'When did she ...'

'That evening, when you and Anil were in your farmhouse. Anita was supposed to join you later since she wanted to discuss some business issue with Anil. But unknown to you or Anil, she had arrived early.

'She parked her car and slipped into the house using her key. That was the day Anil wanted to come clean with you. She must have heard you both upstairs. But she could make out from the conversation that he hadn't, as yet. When Anil came out, she confronted him and probably begged him not to do it. She must have decided that there was only one way to stop him. She knew about the golf set in the closet. She could also see that Anil was a little drunk. She took out a club and as he started down the stairs, she struck the back of his head and he fell. It is not clear whether the blow or the fall led to your husband's death. Either way, it's murder.'

Wow! It was like Pari had dictated the story and the rest of these fools had performed it ... like puppets!

'Go on, Inspector.'

'Well, after that Anita took the golf club and put it in the boot of her car. She was smart. She waited for the phone call she was sure would come. And it did, fifteen minutes later, on her cellphone. She waited another fifteen minutes and came in to console you. When the police arrived, the murder weapon was safely in her car. What she didn't know was that the carpet fibers in a car's boot are very rough and can pick up microscopic particles of blood. Of course, she has got rid of the golf club by now, but under interrogation, even hardened criminals break.'

When he left, she spun around to face Pari, who had been sitting in her favourite easy chair through the meeting. Pari did not gloat for even a minute.

'I want my gift,' she said.

Preeti was taken by surprise. 'Now? I mean isn't it too early to be ... who?' she asked.

'Navin Bhatia,' Pari said.

'Oh god, Pari. Please don't make me ... There's too much on my mind.'

'It's the agreement, Larla, and don't pretend you don't enjoy it.'

Pari was right. It was a small price to pay in return for genius, for access to the storehouse of the stories in Pari's head. Pari, because of her condition, could never have a relationship with a man. But that did not mean she didn't have needs, desires. And all she wanted in return for her stories was for Preeti to go out there and look for a man who fit the description of the latest hero in her latest story. And have an affair with him. Pari would then get off on the explicit narration of the exploit by Preeti.

Navin Bhatia was a jet-setting business tycoon. He was also the inspiration behind the hero in Preeti's latest bestseller.

She would call him tonight and arrange a meeting on his yacht. It had to be discreet. She'd held it off long enough to pique his curiosity.

Pari's silk scarf would accompany her as it had on many such excursions. Only then did she feel part of the whole experience. Her body tingled with anticipation.

Pari knows me too well. I didn't realize how much I miss the physical intimacy. She looked across to the easy chair at Pari and thought, The years have only brought us closer. She is a part of my first conscious memory. She had a hazy recollection of a flea market but couldn't make out the people, just the presence of her mother, a smaller and meaner entity – must be Anita– and suddenly by her side was Pari ... just like that. She remembered the fears and helplessness of their childhood. She had not spoken a word till she was four. Their parents were convinced that she would also turn out like Pari, deaf and mute.

But then she had uttered her first stuttering syllables and left Pari alone, forever, in the darkness. For many years after that, Anita used to scare her by saying that she could make her a deaf–mute again, like Pari.

'You can have the first chapter by tomorrow, but you have to go to Navin Bhatia tonight.' Pari broke into her thoughts.

'Won't it be too soon for the book?'

'It has to hit the stands while the story is still hot to get maximum mileage.'

Pari's forecast for the book was spot on. When it came out six months later, it notched up record sales in the first week. The public's heightened appetite was obviously a result of the scandal. The story of the betrayal of a sister and wife made for heart-wrenching reading. Suddenly Preeti was the writer extraordinaire again. Film rights were being negotiated.

'Do you see it now, darling? We're free. We're capable

of whipping up inspiration for ourselves whenever we want.' Pari's eyes were gleaming.

Anita's case was in the court. Bail denied. Only Preeti's millions could buy the kind of legal help required to free Anita. And Preeti had let it be known that she would want Anita to get the maximum sentence.

Things couldn't be better, though occasionally, a panicked sense of fear and insecurity would clutch at Preeti. Despite all the consolations that Pari offered her, she would withdraw into herself and refuse to have anything to do with the world, sometimes for several days at a time. On one such occasion, angry and frustrated with her behaviour, Pari wrote and signed a confession, taking responsibility for her part in the deed, then sealed it and gave it to Preeti. For a while, this served to calm Preeti. Pari's confidence finally convinced her that nothing could go wrong.

Six months after the release of her book, a police car pulled into the driveway. Pari met them in the verandah. Chief Patil was flanked by three assistants. He greeted her, she noted, with the same expression of pity.

Preeti couldn't help the irritation in her voice.

'Is this a social call, Chief?'

'Er ... yes, I suppose so.' The tone was still irritatingly sombre.

Oh! Get over it, man! Your supercilious pity, keep it for yourself. It's you who has been had! she thought.

'Oh! But I don't mind these visits at all. All the policemen I've met have been nice.'

'I know they have. One more than others.'

She froze. The same fear that she'd thought gone, moved up to her throat.

'Isn't that so, madam? Wasn't the recipient of your affections a certain police officer? It happened a few years back, but not long enough for you to have forgotten. He hasn't. He told us himself.'

They knew! Oh, god! She should have stood up to Pari. For once in her life she should have not paid heed to her insanity.

'What are you talking about, officer?' she managed to break the silence.

'Let me begin at the beginning,' Patil said.

She looked beyond him at the easy chair, at Pari. If Pari knew that their scheme was coming apart, she didn't show it. She just stared at Preeti, her eyes lifeless and inscrutable.

'You know, ma'am, I'm not a very imaginative person. I know that about myself, so I don't count on imagination or even instinct. And it works for me. It makes me stick to the facts. To dig out all the facts of this case, we started researching all your backgrounds. I'd ordered you all to be followed for a couple of weeks after the murder. I was shocked to find that a few days after the supposedly tragic events, you were out one night for what could only be described as a romantic rendezvous with a certain Navin Bhatia, a well-known playboy. Fact is, it was the quickest recovery I'd seen in any widow. I couldn't understand why you couldn't have waited?

'After that I was sure you'd done it, but I needed proof ... and I had to act out the charade of arresting your sister. Because of your profile, there was great pressure to solve the case quickly. You, it seems, decided to do this several months ago. You designed a beautiful case for us. You knew that we'd suspect a romantic involvement between your sister and your husband. We made a list of all their travels, where they could have been alone. You bought airline tickets and planted the receipts in Anil's files, you knew that airlines keep a record only for six months. You wrote a couple of romantic notes from Anil – nothing elaborate – just to give us a hint of an extramarital affair. You then ripped those pages from his notepad. You knew that we have a technique of being able to lift impressions off a pad. I'm not surprised that you can copy your husband's writing. A lot of women can.

'That evening, you knew that Anita would be coming to your house later. You opened a bottle of wine, poured a glass for yourself and Anil, lit some incense and went in for a bath.

'It was no ordinary incense. Making incense is your hobby and this one was laced with a sleep-inducing drug. Just the powder of a handful of sleeping pills for which you have a prescription.

'It took me a long time to figure out why the drug. You're a frail person and your husband was a big man. Handling him later would be easier if he was drugged. You couldn't mix something in his wine because that would show up in the autopsy. You must have thought, who would analyse the ash that was left of the incense? You would have been right, normally nobody with any imagination. I told you I have none. I sent samples of everything in the room for chemical analysis.

'You then struck him with the golf club and he fell to his death. When Anita arrived, you got your chance. You wiped some of the blood off in the boot of her car. Just enough to show up in a microscopic examination. Am I correct so far?'

She felt the need to do something ... Move or be still like Pari ... Don't let your face betray you.

He cleared his throat. 'I realized during the investigation that you probably know more about forensics than a lot of cops. The officer you were involved with was a forensic expert, wasn't he? You know that the police use tracker dogs and you still had the murder weapon in the house. But there's a way around that. It's simple: a little ground pepper sprinkled in the vicinity and the dogs are desensitized. But, ma'am, even pepper leaves traces on a carpet.'

She stared at Pari. Deaf, mute, deaf, mute. Pari seemed to be taunting her. Was she crazy?

'You know, thirty years on the force and I've never seen such convincing evidence. But that was the problem, lady. It was just too pat. Too much like a script. The difference between writing fiction and real life, I suppose.

'Even so, all this evidence is not enough. All this will give you a bestseller, but not a conviction. Without the murder weapon, there's no case.'

She saw a glimmer of light. Maybe they would be okay. That was Pari's brilliance. They would never find their murder weapon.

'So we waited till we found it.'

The rest of his words seemed to fade away. She couldn't hear a thing. She knew that she was doomed. There never had been any pity in that voice. Or had there? And if it was sympathy, what about her was pitiable?

Suddenly his voice was clear.

'There was always the matter of the hidden golf club, the murder weapon. Some time back you made it known that you couldn't bear to have your husband's things around the house so you decided to give them away to a charity ... including his golf set. Your police friend told you everything about forensics, but nothing about routine legwork. That's the most unromantic part of our job, but in my view the most crucial. I've had a team checking everything coming in and going out of your house, including trash, for the past many months. We were shocked to find that the golf set you gave away now contained a full set of clubs – all fourteen, including the one used in the murder.

'It was a brilliant hiding place and if we hadn't been on to you, we would never have found it and there could have been no case against you.'

They had been on to her! But she'd fooled them ... they were sheep ... Pari had sworn that nothing could go wrong ... they had outwitted Pari?

Chief Patil's next words seemed to reach her through a haze.

'You are under arrest as per section 302 of the penal code, for murder.'

No! She wouldn't go alone. Pari was equally responsible! It was all her idea.

'Tell them!' she was screaming now. 'Tell them it was your idea! It wasn't just me.'

But there was no response from Pari. She just sat there, observing. Was she smiling? Was Pari with them? Had she been given immunity to turn her in?

But wait, she still had Pari's written confession.

She moved to the safe to get the letter. She got the incriminating letter out of the safe and waved it triumphantly. She handed it to the chief. He stared at it, looking confused.

What was he doing? Read it, goddamit!

She snatched it out of his hands. It was blank.

She'd been betrayed all her life by everybody. Now even Pari. Why had Pari done it? Was it the will? Her money? Had she decided to be free?

Suddenly she was calm. She moved to the desk and picked up the ornamental khukhri. It was still razor sharp.

Before the officers could stop her, she threw herself across the room at the easy chair. She thrust the knife into Pari repeatedly, with each blow sobbing and flinching with pain as if she was tearing at herself.

'Die!' she screamed. 'Die!'

She then turned the knife on herself.

The carnage was terrible to look at.

The old faded rag doll with burn marks on its face had fallen off the easy chair to the floor and lay in shreds.

Lying next to her was Preeti. Her blood ran in a rivulet on the marble floor, soaking and mingling intimately with the remains of the doll.

Twenty20

Alok looked at the pulsating creature on the screen. 'Oh, yeah, baby! Go do your magic!'

He pressed 'enter'.

With a whoop, the figure telescoped into the great digital beyond.

The 'worm', as the creature was called, dragged its binary body through the waves, innocently merging with its environment till it reached its target – the centralized computer system of a bank.

There, it changed shape and form, deliberately fragmenting its body into bit-sized pieces to enter the heavily guarded portals. Banks had the best safeguards that money could buy. But this worm was the creation of one of the craftiest minds in the trade. Unrecognizable in its piecemeal form, it fooled the gatekeepers, the firewalls, and slid its decapitated body into the stream of digital traffic.

Once through the gates, the head beckoned the other parts and in a hundredth of a second, the worm had assumed its original form. Its antennae were out and the cyber marauder was ready to do its dirty deed.

Alok now had access to the bank's mainframe computer. He started out by transferring enormous amounts of money into a dummy account. Next he transferred blue chip stocks to his portfolio. In ten minutes, the nineteen year old had created wealth that these account holders had accumulated in their lifetimes. For a few minutes he gloated over his net worth. Alok's empire was only virtual, of course. He'd done this a dozen times only to finally hit 'delete' and sacrifice his creations. His passion was the romance and buzz of adventure as he forayed into the cyber world and matched his skill with the best safeguards that computer companies had invented.

Paradoxically, the young man had just dropped out of a renowned computer application programme from the University of San Francisco. In the time-honoured tradition of Indian families, Alok had been sponsored by a cousin who had made it big during the IT boom in the Bay area. But to the disappointment of the whole family, Alok had given up midway and dropped out without a degree – the first step to an American green card.

An only child born to parents in their middle age, Alok was doomed to be a loner from the start. Alok had just two real interests in life. Rated number one was 'cybertripping'. A distant second was the Twenty20 version of cricket. He wasn't interested in the tedious assignments of a formal education. And they didn't follow cricket in America.

To the world, Alok was just another computer geek. In reality, the boy possessed a rare gift. He was a hacker. One of the few who had made hacking an art form.

He heard his cellphone beep. That rarely happened since the lonely world of cyber geekdom wasn't good for socializing. This call was from one of his few admirers. An aspiring hacker who looked up to Alok as an incredible treasure trove of tricks and tools.

The underground bunker complex, thirty kilometres from New Delhi belonged to another era. The elaborate warren of tunnels had been built by the British after the great mutiny in 1857 and left to rot years ago. Only the entrance to one such tunnel showed signs of restoration. It was the home of the 1st Advanced Signal Regiment of the Indian Army.

This subterranean world had much going for it. The robust construction required little maintenance. It was easy to guard. But its greatest advantage was that its thick walls cocooned the delicate equipment and activity inside from any electronic eavesdropping.

Computerization had come late to traditional Third World organizations like the Indian Army. But soon the world had seen that the Indian brain was remarkably deft at software application. After the initial scepticism, the army lapped up cyber tech with parade-ground vigour. Apart from centralized control at the touch of a button, it made redundant, in a single stroke, hundreds of clerks and storekeepers who were part of the rather large tail as compared to the teeth of the army. It made good sense and great press.

The 1st Advanced Signal Regiment handled the bulk of the army's state-of-the-art computers. From clusters of work stations, operators controlled every activity of the second largest army in the world. The workforce stationed there called it simply 'the bunker'. Communications, postings, war games, supplies, ammunition stores, even the hush-hush 'nuclear assets' – the bunker controlled them all.

To most of its inmates the bunker was a dream come true. The work hours were easy and the air-conditioning a blessed relief from the Indian summer. Young men had been educated on the army's account to operate high-tech computers. A skill that could prove lucrative in the civilian world.

Not everyone though, found the assignment at the bunker to their liking. Least of all, the commander of the facility, Colonel Raj Sondhi. A paratrooper officer with a frontline regiment and a shot at the gold leaves of a general, his selection to command the bunker had come as a shock. Neither he nor his peers had heard of the unit.

In the tradition of the army, upcoming officers who might amount to something were tagged at an early stage. Those who had a chance of 'making it', the army's euphemism for becoming a general, were given key assignments.

Sondhi's heart had been set on commanding a regiment of five hundred paratroopers. It had taken him quite a while to grasp the importance of the bunker.

But when he did, he commanded it with great flair. Problem was, he could find no tangible way to showcase his success. Other field assignments were graded at exercises and war games. The army had still not found a way to pit and test banks of computers against each other.

Sondhi's greatest desire was to get the coveted gold leaves, the accompanying salaams and the power that came with a general's rank. The exotic designations that generals were given were like symphonies to his ears. To get there, one not only needed to be good, but importantly, had to broadcast it too. He needed to come up with a way to make them sit up and take notice.

Sondhi got his break on his next vacation. He was visiting family in Delhi. His gawky teenage nephew, a boy whose presence he found embarrassing, had found an interesting hobby. He had, in his own words, turned 'cyber rouge'. The boy went on to tell him that a talented hacker could penetrate any computer system and rummage around or plant bugs to control or collapse the host system. Of course, the more secure systems had strong defenses, but even those could be breached.

Had Sondhi not recently been given the run of the army's computers, he would have dismissed his nephew's words as mere pap.

'Can your hacker friends get through the best kinds of firewalls?'

'Oh, sure. Maybe not my buddies but a super hacker can.'

'Do you know any such fellow? A super hacker?'

He saw the boy hesitate.

'Don't worry, I won't get him into trouble. I just want to meet him ... You know, maybe over beer at the club. You chaps drink beer, right?'

The boy shrugged. 'I know such a guy.'

'Okay. Call him.'

That's how Alok came to work for the army. Strictly temporary, he was told ... only as an experiment. Since rules of admittance to the bunker were strict, Alok was fitted out with army gear. The camouflage fatigues hung from his rail-thin frame. His spiked hair when released from the confines of a beret stood in all directions, like errant antennae. His clumsy efforts to shine his boots resulted in a weird smudgy effect. He was, as a result, the picture of unmilitaryness. Luckily, his baby-fine facial hair saved him the daily hassle of shaving.

For Alok, the strict protocol and discipline of the army made this world, in his words, 'totally bizzaro'. He didn't know how he'd fit in. The colonel hadn't been very clear what exactly the army wanted of him.

He soon realized that these were strictly regimented and drilled men. Any creative thoughts would have to be his own. He didn't mind at all. It was the ultimate in jobs, playing a nonstop video game against a very real enemy. Hackers were considered to be intrusive, predatory, and for the most part, illegit. The army was giving him a chance to show off his talent openly. He was a knight sallying forth into cyberspace to engage his nation's foes. Wow!

Alok's first 'hack attack' was a demonstration of sorts. For if Alok was being tested, then so was Col. Sondhi, by his bosses. So far, all they knew was that on a hunch Sondhi had hired a geeky kid.

Alok decided to first study the systems of their archenemy – Pakistan. When he was sure that they had nothing he hadn't cracked before, he moved. For the demo attack, he decided to tap into the computer systems of the logistics branch of the Pakistan army. The operation he had designed to exhibit his talent was brilliant in its simplicity. It would generate a false request to the supply depot so that the requesting unit received equipment that it had no use for.

'How do we figure out if the mission has been successful?' Sondhi asked.

'You've got to judge a hack by two things. One, the creativity the hacker shows and the other, by the cost of damage inflicted.'

Having said this, Alok took his time to select the target.

After several hours of scrolling through hundreds of requests, he hit upon one that made him smile.

A request had been made from a Pak army unit in the Siachen Glacier, the highest battleground in the world, for protective covers for their rifles since heavy snowstorms were causing a lot of damage.

Alok decided to substitute the rifle covers for something else. He was able to access and scroll through the complete listing in the Pakistan army's inventory. He stopped at an item.

To accomplish the hack, Alok had to travel along the same virtual route that such a request normally travelled. Needless to say, the Pakistan army's computer systems was not accessible to the outside world. But like most systems, it had an Achilles heel. The guardians of a system are its firewalls and entry codes. In this case, the codes had been designed by an American company – as are most safeguards in the business. Alok, after his stint in the US, could crack any of them.

He started by 'rooting' himself to their computers. Rooting is akin to hypnotizing a system. He could then access any programme and manipulate the computers to obey his commands.

Alok was able to make and move his request through the network and clear it along all the checks that the Pakistanis had installed.

He generated shipping documents for his request. The unit was stationed deep in the Siachen Glacier at a height of 16,000 feet above sea level. To get to the unit, first a Pakistan air force Hercules aircraft would take off from its base in Rawalpindi and fly north 600 kilometres to Skardu airfield. From there, the load would be transferred to a helicopter which would fly for two hours through tough Himalayan terrain to make the final drop. The computer-generated paperwork to requisition such an expedition had to be perfect.

It was only when he dotted his last virtual 'i' and crossed the last digital 't' that Alok eased back in his seat and whistled the '*I love this game*' theme they played at Twenty20 matches. He turned to find a dozen spectators watching his performance. He felt the first doubts creep in. He brushed them aside. This is how players must feel in the dugouts, he thought. Well this was his dugout and man, was he batting for Team India!

'Is it over?' Sondhi asked.

He nodded.

'How will we know that it worked?'

'I thought about that. I've also rooted their communications system. What I've done will raise a serious stink. If we monitor all their communication out of Siachen, we'll pick it up.'

Sondhi stared at the nineteen-year-old's face.

'Are you saying that you can pick up all their messages out of Siachen Glacier?'

'Sure ... It's all in code, but the key to the code is also in the computers.'

Sondhi was shocked. The two countries had been locked in a bloody conflict at Siachen for twenty-eight years. It had taken the Indian Army dozens of listening posts and hundreds of man hours to intercept Pakistani communication from Siachen. Even then it was never more than fifty per cent effective.

This boy had managed to do all that in a few hours. Incredible!

'Why do you say this will raise a stink?'

'Oh ho ...' Alok's smile turned wicked. 'Now this is crazy stuff. The request of that unit was rifle covers. I wanted to rock their world, so I browsed through their stock piles till I came to an interesting entry. Do you know that the Paki army also stores condoms?'

'Yes, it's not unusual. So do we ... and a lot of other armies. Soldiers are away from their women for months. It's to prevent disease.'

'Is that right? Anyway, that forward unit is probably hundreds of miles from any women, but it's going to get a ton of condoms. Covers, all right, but not for their rifles, eh?'

The entire group dissolved into laughter. A few even clapped. Alok sat back and soaked it all in.

Twenty-four hours later, Alok held up a computer printout. It was a copy of the message that the commander of the Pakistani unit had sent to the supply depot. The man was obviously Punjabi and had used the choicest expletives, something the language is really suited for, all in correct military code.

Alok turned to the rest of the staff.

'You know, I worked out that it costs a bomb to air lift cargo to the glacier. That useless little courier just cost them a few lakhs.'

Sondhi studied the boy from the back of the room. His intuition had been right. This geeky youth was the key. The last Indo-Pak conflict had taken place in Kargil in 1999. Frustratingly, Sondhi had been posted to the eastern front then and had missed all the action. And the medals.

This boy had just become the most destructive weapon of the Indian Army and through him, Sondhi's career could take the fast track.

Overnight Alok became as much of a celebrity as this hush-hush world allowed. He wanted to shout his success to everyone he met. He itched to tell all, especially the cool women in his college who had been oblivious to his existence, and the jocks who treated him with utter contempt. But for now he had to be content with the praise he received from the army top brass. In the upper echelons of the army he had become everyone's favourite kid. He was the showpiece of every senior rank trying to impress his bosses. Sondhi felt his protégé slip from his grasp as more officers raced to attach themselves to the idea of Alok.

For the next few days, Alok worked on improving his methods. Soon he grew tired of the same disruption-of-supplies-and-maintenance jobs. By now he had rummaged through the entire system of the Pakistan military. He wanted to up the ante and hit a high-value target. Headquarters were a bit nervous about this because if it was traced back to them it would be considered a definitive act of war. Though others not connected to Alok's project turned down the idea, Sondhi and his boss, a major general, were riding high on Alok's success. A high-value operation would give their careers a huge fillip. They managed to bulldoze the idea through.

Executing a hack at the bunker had now become a major theatrical event. Although the main player was only Alok, the room was cramped with officers who had got themselves connected to this operation. And though the words 'hack attack' were emblazoned in orange on Alok's khakis, his work was christened with a serious military title: Digital Strike Cell.

Alok was given the run of any computer system or equipment he wanted during the hack. A couple of junior officers were given to him as deputies. They were both army computer specialists but for all the understanding they had of hacking, they might as well be sharpening their pencils and stacking his stationery. They all wore headsets with boom mikes for instant communication, but more because Alok wanted the team to look cutting edge.

And though everything was played on the speakers for everyone in the room to hear, Alok knew that most people including his assistants had no idea about the cyber world. He had realized years back that people didn't know and didn't care how much personal information is left behind like a footprint when they browse the net. Computer manufacturers didn't care either about the digital trail their systems left when they were used. All this neglect made a hacker's job that much easier.

While targeting a major secure system, Alok had to electronically assume the identity of someone who was authorized to command the computer.

'Okay guys, here we go,' he said.

'Open the channel,' he told his assistant. Opening a channel was like making a surgical incision, an entry point.

Next, Alok loaded a decoy into the host computer. This decoy was a file that looked deceptively like something the system was used to. This was called a Trojan horse. In the slipstream of this horse, Alok's masterpiece – the worm – would slip in. Inserting this worm was like getting the house keys.

While most of the gathering in the bunker had no idea what young Alok's target was, the top brass including Sondhi did, and they were on edge.

Today Alok was not tampering with Pakistani supplies or routine maintenance schedules. He had infiltrated the main computer of the Pakistan air force and had changed the entire electronic map settings for a flight of F-16 fighter planes from Sargodha airbase. Electronic maps were fed into the computers of the fighters to navigate them through their practice flights. With a wrong map the flight would miss its practice targets completely.

A day later, the Pakistani air force communications channels were choked with this incident.

'That's for Johannesburg!' Alok whooped.

India had narrowly lost to Pakistan in the Twenty20 cricket series in South Africa that week.

Two weeks later, Alok sat at his station in the bunker. The army had formally hired him as a consultant. Though the money was not great, Alok found the thrill of the job and the admiration of these tough military men intoxicating.

It was 2 a.m. and he had just started a minor hack: a disruption of maintenance schedules of a Pakistani tank brigade. Why was it taking so long? The ones he had done earlier had been far more complex than this. Then suddenly the entire screen went blank. Alok stared dumbstruck at the blackness. Before he could react, he saw a figure appear in the top right corner of the screen. It was a caricature of an Arab in traditional getup. The figure grew larger and did a little jig as it whooshed around his screen. Alok watched mesmerized. What the hell was going on?

The figure stopped in the middle of the screen, did a little bow and rolled out a rug. The pattern on the rug was a matrix of the numbers, zero and ones, the basic building blocks of all computer languages. Smack in the middle of the rug was inscribed the word 'Sheikh'.

Alok watched as the worm he had inserted into the

Pakistani network suddenly appeared looking torn and mangled. The Arab, now wielding a sword, filled more and more of the screen. With a jerk Alok reached for the power switch to crash his own system before the 'Sheikh' struck home and did whatever damage its creator intended.

Alok's first instinct was to keep quiet about what had happened. But then, as the horrible fact became clearer, he knew he had to tell.

'What do you mean they've hired themselves a hacker?' the colonel yelled.

'That's the only explanation, sir. After all these attacks, they'd have to be dumb to not know that their systems were being hacked.'

'The boy is right, Raj. It was inevitable that they would realize what was going on.' Sondhi's boss looked thoughtfully at Alok.

'I was expecting something like this. The question now is, son, can you take their hacker on?'

'Sure, sir. Whatever he does, I can do better.'

'Great! Then we're still one step ahead. As they say in sports, Alok, let the games begin!'

'Yes, sir!' Alok brought his hand up in a salute for the first time.

In the next few days, Alok realized that his claim to one-upmanship was becoming increasingly doubtful. Their guy, he had to grudgingly admit, was good. He was blocking all of Alok's attacks and Alok was fast running out of tricks. He could feel he was losing favour with his military masters.

Initially his rival had only been blocking Alok's

efforts, but after a week the officer in charge of communications at the bunker reported that a lot of his computer files were being activated by an intruder. Alok had been in the dog house with his bosses. He leapt at this chance to redeem himself. He used all his expertise to neutralize the hack.

The situation soon reached a stalemate. Like the Indo-Pak situation on any frontier, from Kashmir to Siachen and the Kutch, it became a standoff.

Late one night Alok sat at his station, staring at the screen and wondering if there was some new move he could try. Suddenly the Sheikh appeared on his screen. Before he could jump to switch off his system, he saw that the figure was holding a message. He looked around to make sure he was alone. He clicked on the message. It was from the other guy.

'Hey there, are you the Cyber dude? Wanted to talk about our situation. You interested? My name is Sheikh, what's yours?'

This was unbelievable. This other guy wanted to talk to him! He didn't know if he should be doing this. Was this treason? Those army types might just march him behind the bunker and shoot him.

Another message appeared on the screen.

'Tell me, are your military types as stiff-assed as mine?'

Wow! This was cool. The guy was completely irreverent.

Over the next few days the two hackers set up a private little chat channel. They soon realized that they were both nineteen years old and apart from cybertripping, they were die hard Twenty20 fans. Most of their conversations were bitching sessions about their bosses and intense discussions on Twenty20 cricket.

'I think Sehwag is the most destructive batsman in the world,' Alok wrote.

'Are you nuts, man? There's no one to touch Afridi! Remember Lahore 2007?'

Soon Sheikh's queries became more personal.

'What's your story with women, my friend? Do you go out a lot? Or is there one who has holstered your pistol?!! Ha ha!'

'Chicks and me don't mix, dude. There are lots of fish in the sea but they've all slipped my hook.'

'Hey ... my advice, change your technique. Drop the hook and cast a NET!'

Alok grinned at that.

Of the two, Sheikh was the more proactive one, not afraid to take their friendship up a notch.

Alok didn't remember this later, but it all started as Sheikh's idea.

Sheikh made an offer of truce for mutual gain.

'I hope you realize that if we keep blocking each other, our bosses are soon going to forget our value. I suggest that you let some of my attacks go through and I'll let some of yours. That way the game is still on and we're still in it.'

Alok was shocked. This was crazy. Hell, this was like match fixing. But he realized that Sheikh was right. He could already feel Colonel Sondhi and the others cooling off a little towards him.

He agreed.

Over the next couple of months the two of them carefully choreographed their moves.

Suddenly Alok was the wonder weapon again.

'I told you so. Our armies are happiest with a stalemate,' Sheikh wrote.

A few months later, Sheikh made another offer.

'These guys pay me a pittance. I'm sure you don't make too much either. I've got a plan to milk these buggers.'

Sheikh's plan was to set up a fictitious bank account in Dubai in both their names. Then basically prey on the natural insecurities of both the Indian and Pakistani top brass to let them buy high-end software and programmes from dummy sellers. And siphon the money off to the account in Dubai.

There was nothing in the market to suit their needs anyway. Hacking was too mysterious a science. Bits and pieces of dozens of programmes had to be assembled by the hacker. This gave them the freedom to charge whatever prices they desired. Often they hacked into their respective accounts department's computers to see what amount had been sanctioned under the 'cyber warfare' heading. They would then bill a figure just under that amount.

'Let's do it for six months. Anything more and the chances of getting caught are high. That's also the date for the next Indo-Pak series. We'll meet up in Dubai and split the money, watch the match and never go back to these jobs again.'

Alok thought about it for a couple of days. What finally clinched it for him was something he'd overheard. Sondhi had been pressing him to train the two assistants the army had given him. Just in case he ever fell sick. Alok came to know that the plan was to replace him as soon as they were ready.

Once again, Sheikh was proved right. Both the armies had access to limitless funds. The search for cutting edge and mostly mythical software became the new arms race.

Thousands of dollars were being deposited in their account on a weekly basis.

'We'll meet at the Irish Village in Dubai. It's a great party place. I've informed the bank that we'll be visiting. I've booked two FRONT ROW SEATS for the Twenty20 match. Cheers!'

'Hey, I'll be wearing my "HACK ATTACK" T-shirt, but how will I recognize you?' Alok asked.

'We'll be the only geeks carrying laptops at the Irish Village! I'll look for your T-shirt.'

The Air India and Pakistan International Airways flights land in Dubai within minutes of each other. They dock at adjacent gates. Hundreds of shoppers and migrant workers from both the countries walk a few metres and merge into one large stream heading for immigration. It's difficult to make out who is from which country.

Alok was waiting at the Irish Village. Sheikh was right. This was one great party place, man!

Sharply dressed men and hot women from a dozen countries flooded out of music-filled pubs and bistros on to the streets. There was laughter and the electric buzz of raw promise. He felt hesitant to enter the place in his Cotton World linen jacket.

'Who cares!' he said to himself and walked in, hands in his pockets.

His twentieth birthday was that month. Coincidently, so was Sheikh's. This would be a good place to celebrate.

What if Sheikh never showed up? What if it was all a hoax – the ultimate hack?

Alok heard a shuffle behind him and a tap on his shoulder.

He turned to find himself looking at a pair of eyes behind thick glasses exactly like his. Traditional salwar-kameez and a headscarf.

She smiled at him.

'Hi ... I'm Sheikh.'

She looked as awkward as he felt.

'Hi.' Then silence.

'Uh ... should we get a beer?' Alok finally said.

'Uh ... I don't drink.'

'Oh, of course. Coffee then?'

'Yeah, I know a great place for Java.'

As they settled down, she pulled off her headscarf, folded it neatly and put it into her satchel. She pushed back an unruly mop of long spiral curls. He noticed her hands. They were really pretty.

She scooped up large pieces of cheese with her soda bread. Talking through mouthfuls, she gave him a precise account of their takings down to the last cent, not forgetting to divide even their present bill. Everything half and half.

He had to admit the macchiato was excellent. As he sucked up the last of it, he asked, 'Now what?'

She looked up.

'What kind of food do you like – Lebanese or Chinese?'

'What do you mean?' he asked, looking at the platter wiped clean.

She laughed. 'Not now, you nut ... I mean the future. Aren't there wars going on everywhere?

'Our next stop could be Israel–Palestine, or China–Taiwan. Even Iran, I hear they're desperate.'

She laughed at his surprised expression and said, 'Come on! Let's play another round, another place ... you take one side, I'll play for the other. As long as people are fighting, we'll be in business. It could be like our very own IPL. Are you game?'

Before he could respond, she jumped up. 'Oh, god! we'll be late for the match. I don't want to miss the toss.'

The Day Tina was Born

Tina was dying. And I think she knew it. I think even a five year old has an innate understanding of death. I knew that she knew because she'd stopped asking for more dolls.

Tina loved Barbie dolls. They spilled out of her cupboard and from under the bed. They were stacked along the walls of her room, but she wanted more. She would place a dozen of them around herself when she played, happily surrounded by a profusion of golden curls and pretty laced-trimmed dresses. In their midst, she stood out even more. That's how beautiful my little girl was.

Don't get me wrong, I know all fathers find their daughters adorable. But I speak now almost as an observer, a man cauterized of emotion by great pain.

Tina had always been an exceptionally gifted child. Her long, honey-brown hair cascaded down to her shoulders, forming a perfect frame for her cherubic face. Her eyes were the clearest, brightest mirrors I'd ever seen. They projected every emotion of hers clearly and instantly. I loved Tina from the moment I set eyes on her.

I would come home from work and kiss her cheeks and rub my face on her creamy skin. She'd cry out from the prickle of my stubble.

'No, Daddy!'

'Okay, I'll go kiss Barbie then.'

She'd fall for it every time.

'No! Kiss me, Daddy! Don't kiss Barbie ... kiss me!'

'You're my baby Barbie,' I'd say and she'd collapse in a giggling fit.

'Where did you buy me from, Daddy?'

'The great store in the ...' We'd point upward together and shout, 'sky!'

And that's where she was headed now ... The great store in the sky. Where do children come from? How do their little bodies have it in them? And how does their littleness have such a big influence on our lives?

I had never been much into kids. Dianne, my wife, hadn't been too keen either. I mean we tolerated with amicable humour our friends' brats, but we never yearned for our own. It suited our brisk professional lifestyles.

Tina was born of a late pregnancy, what they call a precious one. The doctors had made it clear that Dianne could never have another child.

I know you think that's why we were so attached to Tina. I've thought about it a lot, even wished it as a mechanism to help me cope with her loss. Tina was magical, no one could help getting attached to her. But even her magic could have no effect on the poison that was slowly gnawing away at her little body. They called it Alpers' syndrome. A degenerative disease of the brain, it would tighten its stranglehold on her nervous system, leading to a sudden massive stroke. And it would happen in the next few months. I would have to watch her wither and fade away.

Alpers' is incurable, they told us.

That which made her bright and lovely and unique, her brain, was destroying her from within.

Before this I'd never heard of Alpers' syndrome. Apparently, it's an extremely rare disorder that affects kids. The chances of getting it are like one in ten million.

These odds didn't help my child.

For the first few days after Tina was diagnosed, life for us became frantic rounds of hospitals and specialist doctors. Endless tests, reports and analyses. It was a roller-coaster ride of hope and despair with every test and every doctor. The smell of hospitals engulfed our home and we carried it around with us everywhere.

I would wake up each night, if I ever slept at all, sweating, and get up to look at Tina.

Was she all right? Was she still there?

Dianne and I were Catholic. Both our parents lived in Vasai, a Mumbai suburb where the fervour of faith still runs high. But who has the time for religion anymore? Like so many of our generation, we had transferred passion for the church to our professions. We were too busy to be devout.

Our visits to the church were limited to occasional weddings or the odd baptism.

I had always been an optimist. I believed in ethics and hard work. It had served me well. I had a good job in a bank and a super family. It had been a long while since I thought of God.

In the first few days, I had a lot of hope.

'We'll find a way. It'll work out just fine. She'll be the first one to respond to the treatment.'

Or, 'So sorry, there's been a mix up. These reports are not her's.'

I played out these scenarios a hundred times in my head.

'Nothing is going to happen to her. She's ours. Nothing can happen to such a lovely child. All this will just go away.'

It's amazing how strong an instinct denial is.

But you can't smother the voice of reality that keeps reminding you of the terrible truth of this world. Hundreds of lovely children die every day.

You know what utter despair is? Watching a renowned doctor as he reads the reports of your child, his eyes unable to hold yours.

I took time off from work. I wanted to spend every moment with her. As if, by holding on tight, I could rescue her. It was futile though, on a very practical level. After a while, no work equates to no pay and Tina's hospital bills were prohibitive. I hated the time in the morning when I had to wave to her as I drove off to work.

One month before her fifth birthday, we got a card from Tina's school. They knew about her condition, so it must have been sent by a careless clerk from the headmistress's office. Like they do for all the kids at kindergarten, they were having a cake and a clown for her birthday. For the first time, I fell to my knees and wept.

The next day, I went to church.

We live in Andheri. I drive to my office in Colaba. En route, I pass St Michael's Church in Mahim. They say visiting the church on nine successive Wednesdays can grant all your wishes. I had just one.

I began to stop at the church every evening. Dianne would often join me. Our prayers were halting, embarrassed mutterings corroded by disuse and disbelief. Sometimes, when no words would come, I would just stand and stare at the crucifix. I don't know what any of this achieved. I hoped I was somehow persuading God to act. I was trying to beg for the life of my child, sometimes demanding it, but most of the time I was trying to instill life in the creator himself.

But Tina continued to sink. Her medical reports kept getting worse and I began to stop at the church morning and evening.

One evening, a visiting priest led us in a new prayer.

'Mother Mary, help the absent loved ones.

How we miss their presence here,

May thy hand guard and guide them far and near.'

We cried when we heard this. We had almost started to feel her absence. We carried the feeling and soon forgot the prayer. But some of the words lingered.

'Guard and guide them far and near ... far and near.'

How could the absent ones be far and near? Far, I could understand. How could one get them to be near?

A couple of months later, Tina suffered a minor stroke. I knew it was beginning. That evening, as I parked my car outside the church, I noticed a group of children across the street. They were urchins. Mumbai has the highest number of street children in the world. A burst water pipe had attracted them. They splashed about joyously, yelling and laughing at the novelty of running water on their grubby bodies. They were about the same age as Tina. I stopped to watch them play. Tina had everything and they had nothing. They had something, though, that Tina didn't. They had life.

I was about to turn away when I heard something. A whisper carried by the sea breeze. For a moment the sounds of traffic and the city receded as the wind formed words.

'Life provides,' the wind said. 'Life will provide.'

Life will provide.

I don't know if He spoke to me that day. Hell, I don't even know if He exists, but I didn't need to go back into church that day. I'd got my answer.

The next day I drove to Chakala, an area in the city I'd never been to before. It was tough to find parking on the main street. At the end of that street was the Holy Cross Orphanage.

The next two months were hell. With Tina's failing condition, our house slumped into a state of perpetual silence. It affected everyone who visited us. While others descended into gloom, I could sense an approaching calm.

Dianne seemed to have aged ten years. Amidst all this, a strange thought troubled me. Would she ever smile again?

Sometimes I caught her looking at me.

How can you not be as devastated as I am? she seemed to accuse me.

I wanted to grab her and explain to her. But I didn't know how. Even in the most intimate relationships, some paths have to be walked alone. I had to tell her though. Without her, this collaboration could never work.

A month later, Tina went to bed one night and never got up. She'd come and gone as an angel.

Taking her little body to be buried the next day is a feeling I'll carry till my end. After the funeral service, I slipped out.

She was waiting for me.

When the sister in charge gave her tiny hand in mine, she asked, 'Her given name is Kaira. Is that what you want to write in the adoption form?'

'No.'

'Whatever name you choose to give her, she'll adapt. She's only five. Have you thought of a name?'

I nodded.

When I walked in with her, Dianne stared at us for a long time.

'Who's this?' she whispered.

'This is Tina.' I nudged the child forward. I knew that I'd taken a big chance. Dianne may not be ready for what she felt would be a replacement for our child. But how could a person, a parent, ever be ready? 'Adopt the universe,' some saint had once said,' and the universe will adopt you.' I was hoping that Dianne would see it in this little girl's eyes. The need to be loved and nurtured and the power to heal ... both ways.

Dianne looked at me for a long long time. I hoped that like me, she'd discovered how to make absent ones come nearer.

Dianne moved up and threw her arms around the girl. She hugged her tight and for the first time in a year, I saw the beginnings of a smile on her face. They stood like that for a long time, then the heaving sobs stopped.

I saw them go hand in hand, mother and daughter, towards Tina's room. I followed.

When she saw the dolls, I saw her face light up and her mouth formed a perfect 'O' in wonder.

I felt good. Tina was home.

'She looks just like her,' Dianne whispered.

I started to correct her, then stopped. The little girl's toffee skin and skeletal frame were very different from Tina's, but I knew what Dianne was saying. The sameness of every child lay in their eyes.

'Life provides. Life will always provide.'

I don't know if it was He who whispered to me that day. I don't know His plans. I'm confident that I never will. I don't even know if He exists. But I know now that life is full of grace and second chances.

I've moved a step closer to immortality. I've found a way to keep Tina alive, you see.

I've found a way to cheat death.

Acknowledgements

This book owes much to many.

My eternal gratitude to Preeti, Pooja, Sam, Varun, Saki, Kanthi, Samir and Arup – incredible friends who read my early attempts at storytelling with a straight face!

Mita at Siyahi: everyone should have a Mita – agent then and friend now. Nothing can get past on her watch!

The brilliant and fun team at HarperCollins: Karthika, Natasha and Shuka for their generous support and patience with a first timer. Especially Karthika, for her incredible insights and for giving me the title.

To Air India, which for the past eighteen years has given me the best office with a view of the world from 35,000 feet above sea level!